Blackmailed
by the Hero

a Gone Hollywood novel

Julie Particka

Entangled Publishing, LLC
2614 South Timberline Road
Suite 109
Fort Collins, CO 80525
Visit our website at www.entangledpublishing.com.

Brazen is an imprint of Entangled Publishing, LLC. For more information on our titles, visit www.brazenbooks.com.

Edited by Karen Grove
Cover design by Heather Howland
Cover art by Shutterstock

Manufactured in the United States of America

First Edition August 2015

To all the people who have ever knocked me down, and to all of those who have ever propped me up… Thank you.

Chapter One

Dinner break was almost over, and Vicky felt like she hadn't rested at all. As excited as she was about her new career possibilities, working her way up the ladder at Elegant Entertainment was no walk in the park. Phone calls like this from her best friend didn't help, either. She clutched the phone tighter, wishing she hadn't picked up at all. As Jade chattered about all the reasons their deal was important, Vicky remembered the original discussion like it had happened yesterday, rather than over three months ago.

"You've been divorced more than a year, Vicky. It's time for you to get yourself laid."

Vicky rolled her eyes at Jade. "I don't need a man."

"I know, I know, you're on this whole independent woman thing, which I wholeheartedly applaud. You don't *need a man. What you do need is an orgasm."*

"Did you forget BOB? He's given me plenty of orgasms."

"If you can say that with a straight face, you're worse off

than I thought." Jade sipped her vodka cranberry. "It's not the same thing, and you know it."

She did know it. She knew hiding in her apartment and only coming out for work or to hang with Jade wasn't moving forward. No matter how many convincing arguments she could make to the contrary, she'd never been very good at lying to herself. And the truth was, Brandon had shattered her self-esteem to the point that she didn't think she deserved happiness. Much less a career *and* her independence *and* a romantic relationship.

So, she'd prioritized. Career first to gain her independence, and then, if she felt the urge, she'd go looking for love in something vaguely resembling the right place. But she'd stalled out at career. A year in and she was finally on track for her first promotion. It'd take at least four more to get where she wanted to be, but she'd make it. After all, the only thing she had left was her determination to go it alone—something Brandon had said she'd never be able to do.

Once upon a time he'd told her he loved how much she needed him, said it made him feel like her knight in shining armor. Somewhere along the way, though, that love had turned bitter. And from that point forward, he reminded her at every turn that she needed to grow up and take care of herself—among other things.

The other things had eventually led to the divorce, and Vicky had been forced to go it alone. Now she was determined to rise or fall without any knights, thank you very much.

But even this get-a-non-battery-induced-orgasm pact was a way for Jade to take care of her. Everyone had always taken care of her. First Mom, then Evan, then she'd married

Brandon…and now Jade had stepped in on the sex thing. Vicky wanted to bail on the bargain, but as much as her friend had shoved her toward it, she had to admit that sex with no strings was probably a good thing. She didn't want to belong to someone again, and doing this would prove to her that she could have a guy without it being such an all-consuming thing, like her marriage had been. Just sex.

One and done.

Hit it and quit it.

She could totally do that. Just not tonight.

Her boss, Mathew Collins, poked his head out the door and arched a brow. That was her warning. Time to wrap up the call and get back to work. Vicky nodded at him, and he left. "On a deadline, my three months are up in a couple weeks. Got it. I have to get back to work now. I'll see you tomorrow."

Her thumb was on the end button when Jade said, "You know, you're at a big Hollywood party. One would think you could find a guy there to take care of business."

If she wasn't wearing her I'm-the-help uniform, she probably could, but she shouldn't. "Right. And then I'd get fired."

"Only if you got caught."

"*Good night, Jade.*" Vicky disconnected the call and fought the urge to scrub at her face. Looking good was part of her job, so smeared makeup wasn't an option. All too often she wondered if she wouldn't have been better off getting a job at Hooters, but the opportunities for advancement with Elegant Entertainment had been too good to pass up. With this job, she could build a career—and a new life—if she played her cards right, and she wouldn't have to rely on being a pretty face forever.

Too bad the game meant starting as a glorified waitress. Soon, though—soon she'd be taking the next step. No one ever said climbing the ladder would be fun or fast—only that everyone had to do it.

Stowing her phone out of sight, she stood and straightened the black skirt that stopped a good four inches above her knees. God, she hated these parties. Someone needed to tell producers that the waitstaff weren't supposed to be eye candy—they were supposed to be invisible. Instead, they were ogled. Some of the women loved it, but she didn't want to be someone's golden girl anymore. She just wanted to earn her paycheck and go home. Give her a nice wedding or bar mitzvah any day. At least at those, she could be fully clothed.

A couple more months, then I can get into billing. No more short skirts or late parties.

In the kitchen, Vicky picked up a tray of hors d'oeuvres— this time it was foie gras with date puree and pomegranate. Her face twisted into a frown; there went her appetite. People would just have to deal with her growling stomach. Starving or not, goose liver really didn't appeal enough to risk a reprimand for sneaking a couple of them for dinner. When was she going to learn to keep protein bars in her purse?

Plastering a smile on her face, she strode from the kitchen into Saul Mortensen's birthday party. He was a producer, so the place was awash in movie stars, wannabe movie stars, directors, musicians, and who knew who else. Basically she was swimming upstream in a river of the rich and famous. Periodically, she'd pause and offer people food, but she tried

not to notice who she talked to. Every time she met someone's eyes, there was a risk they'd recognize her from the oc-
casions her brother had invited her to attend premieres and
parties with him. And then the whispers would start.

Evan Stone's sister is a waitress?

What is she *doing here?*

It wasn't that she minded being the sister of a movie star;
she just didn't want that to be her identity any more than
she'd wanted Evan footing the bill to keep her in L.A. When
Mom had announced her plan to sell the house and relocate
to the Midwest, Evan had offered to buy the place for Vicky.
A post-divorce gift, he'd called it.

A post-divorce handout, more like.

Nope. Vicky was going to make it on her own, and she
was going to make it in Los Angeles if it killed her. Brandon
had walked away from their life together, but somehow the
idea of leaving felt too much like running—too much like
proving him right. She had no intention of letting him chase
her out of town.

So she did the parties, regardless of how short the skirts
were, and she kept her eyes down to keep people from making the connection to Evan. Her apartment might be tiny,
but it was hers, paid for with her own money, and that was
good enough as far as she was concerned. Another couple
months as waitstaff and she'd be eligible to move into Elegant's billing department. Baby steps. That's all it would
take, and soon enough she would no longer be on the front
lines of the business and she could become invisible, or at
least invisible enough.

She was so busy avoiding line of sight with one of Evan's
ex-girlfriends that her heel caught on a rug and she fell into

the arms of Reed Russell, leading man extraordinaire. She'd never met him before, but Vicky had seen some of his films. He was a decent actor with the body of a runner and a face that looked like it should have been carved from marble. Leave it to her to fall into the arms of one of Hollywood's hottest. Luckily her tray was almost empty, or they both would have smelled like goose liver the rest of the night. And that was something she wasn't sure even he could pull off.

Reed caught the one remaining appetizer as it slid off the tray and held it near her lips. "Foie gras?"

"Sorry, I don't French this early."

His lips quirked at the joke, and she found herself smiling along with him despite herself. Placing the food back on her now steady tray, he stood her upright and said, "How about when you get off later? Interested in some French then?"

He was...hitting on her? Vicky cast a covert glance around. There were at least a hundred eligible women at this party, most of whom would give their left eye to have Reed look at them. Why the hell would he be flirting with a wait-ress? "Sorry, but you know I'm part of the staff, right?" At his shrug, she continued, "My boss has a rule about foreign-language lessons on the job."

"Ah," he said, a twinkle in his green eyes, "but I'm talk-ing about after the job. Something more along the lines of you coming back once everyone else is gone."

Definitely hitting on her. Which was flattering as hell, but not exactly a foreign occurrence. She and Evan had grown up getting more than their share of attention because of their looks, and even here in Hollywood, people sometimes mistook her for an ingénue. But flirting with Reed Russell, no matter how pretty he was, screamed bad idea. Vicky was about to make some excuse to get out of the situation when Jade's reminder came back to haunt her. She only had a few weeks left to fulfill her part of their deal, and Reed would definitely be a one-time thing. He wasn't exactly the type to date a waitress, no matter who her brother was. So, it wasn't really an entanglement situation, and he was incredibly attractive.

If she could just guarantee not getting caught... "How would one go about coming back?"

"Simple. A bunch of us have to be here for a meeting tomorrow morning, so Saul offered to let us stay the night. I'll make sure the slider over there is unlocked." He tipped his head to the left. "My room is down the hall directly next to the door. Third room on the right. No muss. No fuss. No one needs to know a thing."

Though away from the party would have been better, the suggested plan was easy. She'd say too easy, but this wasn't like infiltrating some enemy base to gather intel, it was sex. And clearly she'd been watching too many of Evan's movies lately if she was thinking in those terms. "And getting caught? How do I avoid that?"

"If you wait until the rest of the staff is gone, I can pretty much guarantee this part of the house will be empty. As long as you can be a quiet little kitten while you come back in, I promise to have you purring once you're in my room."

The first part was true enough. Hosts and guests rarely, if ever, stuck around for cleanup. That was Elegant's job. So once everyone else on staff dispersed, getting in would be no problem. The kitten thing, though... She found his confidence sexy as hell, but the not-so-veiled pussy reference? Not as much. Still, he was gorgeous, and the way he was looking at her sent a little trill of excitement down her spine. She bit her lip, leaned in close, and said, "Purr."

Reed's hand slid down her arm, thumb grazing the curve of her breast on the way. "Good kitty. I can't wait to see what other noises you make."

With the way her insides tightened, Vicky had to admit Jade was right. She *did* need to get laid. And a one-and-done with Reed Russell was just about the best option she could see in her future. As he said, no muss, no fuss—just no getting caught. She could totally do that. "I hope you're as good as you claim. I haven't had anyone make me scream in a long time."

"I'm better than that, but I don't like to boast. Though, when you scream, you should know I'll be putting something in your mouth so we don't wake anyone."

Vicky couldn't help the giggle that escaped, but when she saw Mathew heading their way, she realized the time for playful banter had ended. Reed would just have to wait until she finished her shift if he wanted more. "I have to get back to work right now, Mr. Russell, but I hope you don't fall asleep on me later."

She turned to leave, followed only by the whispered words, "There won't be any sleeping involved. I can guarantee that."

On an average day, she'd have given him grief about being so forward, especially with her boss hot on her tail. But today wasn't average. Today was the day she was going to give up the ghost of her ex and finally have sex again. Just get it over and done with so she could close that chapter of her life for good. Jade would get off her back, and Vicky could resume her stay-away-from-relationships-at-all-cost-until-she-got-her-shit-together plan. As long as no one ever found out about her and Reed, it would work out perfectly.

With a little more bounce to her step, she moved through the mass of people and back to the kitchen. She didn't bother noticing what tray she picked up this time—it wasn't like she was going to risk nicking food *and* having sex with a guest. Too bad the not noticing things continued as she left the kitchen. That was when a disturbingly familiar voice made heat rush to all the right places, and she almost dropped the hors d'oeuvres entirely.

"What's the matter, Vicks? Not going to offer an old friend a snack?"

She allowed herself two seconds to close her eyes and collect herself before turning around. Not only had she been discovered, but it was by the one guy she'd prayed never to run into—mainly because she wasn't so sure she'd be able to walk away twice. "Dante. I didn't know you were here."

Her brother's best friend shoved off from the wall and stepped closer. Like most men, he wasn't that much taller than her, only five or six inches above her own five-eight, but all his muscles made him seem like he was towering. Yet he managed to pick up one of the pieces from her new tray without shifting it at all. The finger food nearly disappeared in his big hands, but she caught a glimpse, and recognition kept her grounded, kept her from thinking about other things he could do with those magnificent hands.

Crostini with butternut squash and ricotta.

Dante popped it in his mouth and chewed slowly, watching her as she watched him. Just like always, she found herself unable to turn away, even though she knew better.

Something about the man compelled her to look, whether it was the full lips that begged to be nibbled or the strong jaw with its hint of scruff or the muscles that wouldn't quit... she didn't know. He was so unlike the guys she was normally drawn to that the attraction she'd found curious years ago reached overwhelming now. The urge to move closer was almost impossible to resist; he was like a magnet and she was made of iron. She needed to walk away—and not just because she had a job to do. She'd wanted him for too long. Strong and independent women didn't run to the next knight in shining armor—or tarnished armor in his case, at least according to Evan.

One step back, her feet ready to pivot, she froze again as he said, "I've been here all night, watching you, trying to decide if I should say hello or not."

Nope. A whole lot of nope. The deal she'd made with Jade was for a one-time thing she could walk away from, and that wasn't Dante. He was her kryptonite, the guy who made her *want* to be the damsel in distress, and she couldn't be that anymore. Wouldn't be that anymore—no matter how much her body was screaming *yes*, she had to say no. She wasn't about to belong to him any more than she wanted to belong to Brandon. "Well, I *am* working, so some other time might be better."

"I'm sure your boss won't mind you hanging out here as long as I keep eating his food." He took another piece from the tray. "How have you been?"

It should have been an easy question to answer. For most people it would be, but not for her. And especially not talking to him. All the things she wanted to say were the very things she needed to keep shut inside. Because regardless of what she'd been told, her first instinct with Dante had always been to tell him everything, to trust him, to let him be her rock.

She'd met him a few months before her wedding. She'd gone to visit Evan, and he'd been working out with Dante. They'd talked, she'd been drawn to him, and she'd left, thinking nothing of it. For a couple weeks, she kept running into him, whether alone or out with Brandon. And it was always the same. She'd tried to write it off as just a burgeoning new friendship that might have been more flirty than necessary, but nothing worse than that. Then suddenly Evan had told her to keep her distance.

"Dante's bad news, Vicky. He's my best friend, but you're going to get married soon, and you know what they say about wrestlers."

She hadn't, but she found out. The stories were many and terribly unvaried. Women threw themselves at professional wrestlers, and most of them took advantage as often as they could. It didn't matter if she was single, dating, married…any woman was fair game.

Sure, Dante had moved from wrestling to acting and made the transition better than anyone in Hollywood had expected—his natural charisma drawing in more people than just Vicky—but according to Evan, he was the stereotype. And she was falling prey to it, whether she meant to or not.

That was the last thing she'd wanted in her life when she'd been on the verge of getting married. And it was about the last thing she needed now that she was divorced, no matter how much part of her yearned for him still. Even if sex with him would be amazing—and she had no doubts about that—she wanted a man in her bed for one night. Dante was too much drama, too much of something she'd want forever. With how she felt around him, she'd be sucked in and left with her heart broken all over again when he moved on to the next pretty, shiny thing.

Answering the question at last, she said, "Married, no kids, divorced, moved into my own place, making a go of the single life, and debating switching teams because women are less trouble." That covered all the pertinent details without getting personal at all. Too bad she had to bite her lip to keep from spewing about how lonely she was, from telling him all the horrible things Brandon had said to her over the years, how afraid she was that he'd been right about her all along.

"Funny, you never struck me as a switch hitter." He winked, seemingly oblivious, and grabbed another crostini. "Let's see, to catch you up as quickly…five movies, two more on the way, reality TV series, started a charity, three new tattoos, and a piercing. Speaking of tattoos, have you gotten one of your own yet?"

Tattoos. Maybe she could talk about that since he clearly remembered how much she'd liked his, how she'd traced them with her fingers that day at the gym. She saw the edge of flames peeking from beneath his shirtsleeve and had to clench her fist to keep from reaching out. There was no way she could encourage him to show her more—that would involve fewer clothes and a lot more trouble. She had to answer the question, at least, but more than that was dangerous territory.

And focusing on his professional accomplishments would only serve to remind her exactly how lacking her own life had turned out to be in that area. He'd use that to suck her into a much longer conversation, and she needed to get away from him — mainly because she wanted to get closer.

Maybe the other option would shut him down, make him think her interest had disappeared after so much time. Anyone else would believe it. "Piercing? I've never much been a fan of jewelry on a guy."

. . .

Vicky might have been saying all the things designed to push him away, but she hadn't left. And more than that, she had checked him out, her gaze lingering on his biceps. Dante was just nice enough to pretend not to notice. He wasn't, however, nice enough to let that little jab go without one of his own. "Don't worry, Vicks, I only show the piercing to women I really like, if you get my meaning."

Her gaze shot to his chest. Interesting that she'd think nipples first. Grinning, he leaned toward her and whispered, "You might want to aim a little lower with that X-ray vision."

She tipped her head as if she were going to look at the growing bulge in his jeans, but then snapped it back up. "Yeah. Well, I'm sure the kind of women who flock to you love that sort of thing."

It was almost like the rest of the party had disappeared, and for a moment it was just the two of them, poking at each other. They'd done this when they'd first met, though the snark had been a little less biting then. "Funny, I don't see any birds hovering or diving — just you."

For a long minute, she stood there, staring at him, her breath coming quicker with every second, a flush rising on her tanned skin. Then a voice snapped from behind her, "Stone! Back to work."

Vicky started, as if waking from a dream, spun on her heel, and took off into the crowd. "Sorry, Mr. Collins." She didn't even bother to say good-bye. Dante might have been upset if he hadn't caught her looking back his way a second later.

Hopefully her boss wouldn't notice the same thing. Dante grinned at the guy and held up the last crostini he'd snagged. God, he really didn't want any more of the damn things. "Sorry about that. I was trying to figure out how many of these I could eat before I had to up my workout tomorrow."

"Oh, Mr. Palladino, I didn't realize she was talking to you. Mathew Collins, owner of Elegant Entertainment." Dante shook his proffered hand, then the guy straightened his tie and stepped toward the kitchen. "If you like, I'll get the nutritional information and bring it right back."

"Not necessary, since my crostini crack dealer has disappeared. Thanks, though."

"If there's anything else you need…"

Really, all he wanted was an express ticket to the end of the party. The only reason he'd come was because the host was producing his next movie. Industry politics. Yay. "A bottle of water would be great, if you can point me in the right direction."

The guy dipped his bleached-blond head. "I'll be right back with one, Mr. Palladino." He was gone a second later.

Dante hated when people did this—bowed and scraped like he controlled their next paycheck. He was just a guy who'd clawed his way from nothing and gotten lucky with his career moves more times than he could count. Not that he'd go back and change many things, but he wasn't the kind of star who liked being pandered to. He'd fly coach if not for the fact he took up too much room. Him in those seats was an imposition to anyone sitting next to him. But he could sure as hell pick up a damn water bottle.

The guy was back in less than a minute, handed over the water, and then took off as some other party-related emergency grabbed his attention.

Just as well. Dante didn't really feel like chatting. He made his way from the perch against the wall to a similar spot across the room and watched as Vicky passed through the crowd, offering food or glasses of champagne.

Five years. He hadn't seen or spoken to her in five years, ever since the moment Evan had told him she'd asked for him to leave her alone. She was getting married and his flirting made her uncomfortable.

He hadn't actually meant to flirt at all, but when he found someone he enjoyed talking to, his gregarious nature took over. To some women, being friendly meant flirting. The problem was, in hindsight, he realized he *had* been flirting with Vicky. Not only had he liked her, but after he met the guy she was going to marry, he'd wanted to do anything he could to keep them apart. Her fiancé had been an ass—the kind that ogled other women while Vicky was talking to someone. The kind that treated her like some sort of pretty accessory rather than the smart, vivacious beauty she was.

Maybe Dante didn't deserve her, but she sure as hell had deserved better than that joker.

He'd never been so happy to hear about someone's divorce as he had been when he found out about Vicky.

But he hadn't tracked her down afterward or anything. *Stay away* still meant stay away as far as he was concerned. But then she'd been here, and he'd been here. It was like fate had decided to open a window of opportunity.

Too bad Dante had no clue who was supposed to climb through it or in which direction. All he knew was he didn't want it to close before they found out where the path outside it led.

Chapter Two

The party had officially ended two hours ago. One hour for cleanup while attendees made their way to guest rooms or their vehicles. As soon as party staff was officially released, Vicky pulled her car into the darkest corner she could find… and waited. It seemed like forever before Mathew came out. So long, in fact, that she'd started to wonder if he wasn't breaking the rules about fraternizing as well.

Though technically speaking, a one-night stand wasn't really fraternizing. That would imply some sort of ongoing relationship—as friends or otherwise—and she had no doubt if she really got to know Reed, she wouldn't want anything to do with him. Nope. This was a one-time thing to get her over the post-divorce sex hump and on her way to complete freedom. As an added bonus, he wasn't the kind of guy to leave her with visions of happily ever after in her future. She'd likely see him in the tabloids by the end of the week with some new woman on his arm, proving that she was better off on her own. He was the perfect answer to all her problems.

A much safer answer than Dante could ever be.

When Mathew's car finally drove out through the gate, Vicky let herself breathe a sigh of relief. She stepped into the night air again, the light breeze blowing up her too-short skirt, and wondered if she should take a few minutes to throw on some fresh lipstick or something.

Don't be stupid. He's just looking to get laid, too. It's not like he cares how much effort you put in. He picked you up while you were balancing foie gras on a tray, for crying out loud.

She was overthinking this. It was just sex. She'd been having sex since high school. Surely she could manage this. Slowly, she skirted the mansion, aware of people who had taken the party to some of the upstairs balconies. Fortunately they seemed busy enough they wouldn't notice her.

The slider was indeed unlocked, and though it squealed a little upon opening, no one came running to see who it was. Clearly on party nights, Saul Mortensen recognized people would be going in and out and therefore trusted his security to the men running the gate.

Shit. They're going to see me leave, and it's not like my Acura is exactly the thing a celebrity would drive.

There was no way around that issue, though. Leaving now, she was still lingering later than she should have.

In for a penny, in for a pound…

Third door on the right. Third door on the right. She counted softly as she walked. In front of the door, she paused. Was she supposed to knock? That seemed like a stupid idea, one guaranteed to draw someone's attention.

He'd invited her. Better to just walk in.

With a quick glance down the hall in both directions, she eased open the door, slipped inside, and shut it behind her. The click was so quiet, no one should have heard a sound.

Including Reed.

The room was incredibly dark, with heavy drapes pulled shut over most of the windows. Only the far ones were left open, allowing the moon to cast a dim glow over a sitting area consisting of two chairs and a small table. Turning away, she let her eyes adjust to the darkness. A still form lay on the bed.

Had he fallen asleep? She really didn't know protocol for a situation like this. He'd invited her to come back to his room, but was she supposed to wake him or did asleep mean he'd given up and wasn't interested anymore?

For a moment, she considered leaving, but then she remembered her timeline. Jade would ask tomorrow what, if anything, had happened, and it would be really nice to be able to say the deed was done and their deal was finished.

"Screw it," she muttered to the air. If Reed had planned on her being here by a certain time, he damn well should have said so.

She toed off her shoes, laid her purse on the little table, and unbuttoned her blouse. The next question hit. Did she strip down to nothing or just go for easy access? Considering he was already sleeping, she wasn't banking on more than a quickie anyway, so she decided to go for the latter. Panties off, everything else on. At least she'd worn a cute bra tonight, one with lace edging and a little extra lift. Untucking her shirt, she let it hang open.

Good enough.

The closer she came to his sleeping form, the more her heart started to race. Breathing became more difficult than it had any right to be. Who would have thought approaching a one-night stand would have her getting so excited that her nipples were starting to pucker? While most people didn't think of casual sex as taboo anymore, she still did. This was a journey into the unknown for her. Then again, pretty much everything after the divorce had been. Two years was the longest she'd been single since she was old enough to date. She'd never lived alone. She'd never done her own damn taxes. If she could pull off all that, surely she could climb into bed with a hot man who wanted to have sex with her.

Sleepy seduction. One would think she'd have learned how to do this by now, but it had never really been something her ex was interested in. Wetting her lips, she slid under the covers.

Reed was completely naked. She could feel the press of his bare hip against her thighs, and she shivered. Jade was right, it had been far too long, and she was ready to give him the wake-up call of a lifetime.

Vicky splayed her hand on his chest, reveling in those muscles she'd longed to touch. She knew actors stayed in shape, but this was intense. Even resting as he was, she could feel the change from one set of muscles to the next. He shifted, the leg she'd felt earlier sliding between hers. If she moved just a little, she could rub against him and ease a little bit of the ache building in her clit. She'd really prefer him to do that, though; she'd been taking care of her own needs long enough.

She planted kisses along his chest as her hand inched lower.

He stirred at last. "What the…?"

"Shh, it's just me."

"Vicky?"

Like he'd invited a bunch of women to his room to-night and had to guess which one had actually shown up? Sure. If he'd invited other guests, they'd still be here, and she'd watched the rest of the staff leave without a backward glance. "Who else would it be?"

"I thought you weren't interested," he mumbled, his voice still thick and heavy with sleep.

"You thought wrong." Her lips started to follow the path of her hand, lower and lower on his abdomen, shifting the blankets off both of them. Her fingers raked over his happy trail and wrapped around his shaft. He was huge—big enough she thanked God for the toys Jade had bought her to "keep in shape" with.

Her breath started coming faster as she thought about taking him between her lips. The idea of bringing him fully awake that way had her more excited than she wanted to admit. Imagining him bolting upright as she took him deep into her mouth…

What the…?

She'd been sliding her hand along his length, and this time she'd decided to play with his head a little. Only…there was something there. Two little metal balls. Reed Russell had a penis piercing?

• • •

Dante had been sound asleep, dreaming of Vicky. It wasn't the first time, but it was the first in a long time. Seeing her tonight had brought back every inch of his desire for her. In his dream, she'd come to his room and curled up next to him as if it were the most natural thing in the world.

Which was why, when he felt a presence in his bed, he didn't think it was real.

He was even more certain his imagination was fucking with him when he discovered it was her. Then her hand had wrapped around his cock, and he thought he'd died and gone to some strange sinner's heaven.

She started toying with his apadravya piercing, and shivers raced through his body. That, combined with the idea of being inside her and hearing her call his name as she tightened around him, was almost enough to make him come on the spot. He rolled toward her, wrapping her in his arms. "I told you I only showed the piercing to women I really liked."

Her movements paused for a second, and then she jerked back, thrusting his arms away. In her haste to move, she rolled out of the bed and hit the floor with a thud. "Son of a bitch!"

Dante flicked on the light next to the bed. "Are you okay? What's wrong?"

She pushed herself onto her arms, her shirt falling open to reveal a lacy bra that removed the need for what little bit of imagination he'd utilized for those dreams. A crimson flush raced up her tan skin, coloring her neck and spreading to her cheeks. "I... It's just... You're you, that's what's wrong."

"Vicks, I was me when you snuck in my room and crawled into bed with me." The stammering had been cute, but she had the deer-in-the-headlights look that he knew would have her bolting from the room if he didn't calm her down.

When she stood, her skirt rode up, flashing him a view of her ass that removed even more need for imagination. She had the most adorable birthmark—a slightly darker patch of skin shaped almost like a heart. Damn, was there an inch of her that wasn't perfect? Then she yanked on the fabric, promptly removing the temptation to see how well she fit in his hands. She bit her lip, and the red in her cheeks went even darker. "You were supposed to be Reed. He said this was his room."

Reed? Dante blinked, trying to put two and two together. No matter how much he worked at it, though, the answer didn't make sense. "Reed Russell?"

"Is there another Reed staying here tonight? Speaking of, why are *you* here? And would you please cover up your junk?" She waved a hand at the bed, but the way her nipples were straining against her bra told him that it wasn't anger at him so much as other emotions that made her talk to him like that. Embarrassment for sure, based on the blushing, but it seemed some level of attraction was involved, too.

A glance down showed the sheet was actually covering his cock, but barely. While he didn't plan to push his luck, he wanted to see how far she was willing to twist herself up over this. Besides, so long as she was here, she wasn't with Reed. "You were the one who *un*covered it, so I think I'll leave things as they are. I'm here because Saul called a cast meeting for nine in the morning. It was simpler to spend the night than drive home at two and be back by then. And what the fuck were you planning to do with Reed Russell?"

The color rose even higher, her ears pinking now. Her gaze, however, kept shifting toward his cock, then back to his face. "He asked me to come back."

Jesus. And he'd thought her ex was a tool. Reed Russell was the kind of trouble that needed to come with a warning label and multiple levels of tamper-resistant packaging. The idea of her having sex with him, or even letting him touch her, turned Dante's stomach.

"Bad idea. Didn't you hear any of the stories about what he does to women for rejecting him? Or the ones about the women who've lost their jobs shortly after getting involved with him? You know, the ones that supposedly involved video footage as evidence?"

"Sure." She found her shoes and put them back on, her posture a bit defensive. "I've also heard about how my brother knocked up a bunch of sisters. You know, the ones he never met. Both of us are very well aware how much shit tabloids manufacture when it comes to celebrities."

"Yeah, well, sometimes they don't have to get quite so creative." He remembered all too well finding Jeanie, an extra who had told Reed no. The ass had beaten her and left her on set—naked and bruised—for anyone to discover. Dante had personally driven her to the hospital and held her hand as they collected the rape kit. Jeanie could have sent Reed to prison, but she'd been broke as shit and embarrassed. She'd agreed to keep her mouth shut about what he'd done in exchange for a nice, fat check. She still called Dante sometimes when nightmares woke her in her little house back in Kansas. Far away from her demons, but no matter how much money Reed had given her, she hadn't been able to get far enough.

He grabbed his pants from where he'd tossed them at the end of the bed and yanked them on. "You can do a lot better than Reed Russell, Vicks."

"What? Like you?" She moved to pick up her purse, but in her rush, bumped it off the table. It fell with a crash and the contents scattered. "Damn it."

"Yeah, well you could do a lot worse than me. After all, there's a reason I make a point of only playing heroes." Granted, she knew nothing about his history other than what the general public did. And his friendship with Lee Corbitt and the disaster that followed would never be included in any interviews he was willing to give. He knelt down on the floor as she scooped up her wallet and keys. "Let me help you."

"I don't need any help." She released a sigh and scrubbed at her face, suddenly looking completely exhausted. "I really just need to go home. This was stupid."

Dante tugged on his shirt, then strode toward the door. His bare foot caught on a scrap of lace, and he bent to pick it up. The hard-on that had softened upon discovering Vicky's real plans for the night threatened to come roaring back. He held the fabric toward her. "You might want to take these with you."

"Shit." She snatched her panties from his fingers and stuffed them in her purse. Keys dangling in her hand, she stepped toward the door. "I can see myself out. I don't need an escort."

She might not need one, but he wasn't letting her out of his sight until she was far from Reed's reach. "Too bad. You woke me up. I get the right to lock the door behind you."

She yanked open the door and stepped into the hall, laughing for the first time all night. It was like the five years standing between them vanished for a second, and they were right back to how they used to be. "You're such a jerk sometimes."

"I am. I really am," he said, then she froze, panic eking into her features. Dante followed her line of sight. Mortensen. Crap. He plastered on a smile, doing his level best to act like this was no big deal. "Hey, Saul, have you met Vicky?"

Saul Mortensen frowned, lines of irritation carving deep into his face. "I haven't had the pleasure." Regardless of how polite his words seemed, there was venom behind them. Vicky was breaking house rules. Guests could mingle at their leisure, but Saul detested when they mixed with the staff hired for one of his parties.

Dante nudged her forward. "You know my good friend Evan Stone? Vicky here is his younger sister. I haven't seen her in years, and we were just catching up. I know it's technically against the rules, but I didn't think you'd be upset since we're old friends."

Without another way out, Vicky raised her hand toward Saul and forced a smile. "Nice to meet you. Sorry for hanging around. It was just such a surprise seeing Dante at your party that I didn't want to miss the opportunity to find out what he's been up to. Now that Evan's married and splitting his time between here and Detroit, I don't get nearly as many updates on his friends. I hope you don't mind." She twisted her face into a mask of innocence most starlets couldn't have pulled off.

Saul softened immediately and took her hand. "Of course, Miss Stone. We've had some trouble tonight already, though, so please forgive me, but I must ask you to leave."

"No problem. I was just on my way out anyway."

Dante nodded to him, then walked Vicky out to the

driveway. "You handled that well. I'm glad you played along."

"I didn't think there was much choice. Play along or lose my job. Decisions, decisions." She shifted her hands up and down like they were a scale. Dante chuckled, and she pointed to an Acura in the shadow of some trees. "That's me. I can handle the rest of the walk on my own."

"Or you can let me make sure no one's hiding in the bushes to jump you."

"Right." She stretched the word out like her sarcasm could go on forever, but she didn't argue as they kept walking. Unlocking the door, she cast a glance at him. "Thanks for saving my job back there. I do appreciate it."

Dante nodded, watching as the breeze caught her hair, blowing golden strands across her cheek. "Not a problem. For the most part I even managed to tell the truth. I'm just glad you didn't bend over or the evasion would have been blown by your lack of panties."

Laughing, she brushed the loose hair behind her ear. "Yeah. Thanks for not dropping anything, I guess." She got quiet again, and time seemed to stretch between them. He could almost feel heat pouring off her. Then she said, "I'll... tell Evan you said hi."

As she moved to climb behind the wheel, Dante threw logic and caution to the wind and laid a hand on the door. "If you really want to thank me, you can text and let me know you got home safely."

"Thanks, but I don't need a babysitter."

"Humor me." When she only stared at him, he pulled out his trump card. "If anything happens to you and Evan finds out I was here, he'll have my head."

Sighing she dug her phone from her purse and handed it over. "One text—it'll either say I'm home or that I've been kidnapped. Either way, I'm passing out after I hit send."

"That's all I'm asking." He added his contact info and gave her the phone back. "Drive safely."

"Please." She snorted. "At this time of night I only have the drunks to worry about. Much safer than the traffic." Then she slammed the door and started the engine. She was pulling away before he could think of anything to say.

Probably just as well.

Back in the house, Dante locked the slider and made his way toward his room, pausing as raised voices hit him.

"I don't care how much money your films make, Reed. My home is not your personal whorehouse. If you want to have an orgy, do it on your own time and your own damn property." Saul slammed the door across from Dante's room.

"That was the source of the trouble?" Dante arched a brow at Reed's room.

"Isn't it always?" Saul rubbed his temples like he could chase the pain-in-the-ass actor away. "Three women. One possibly underage. If he wasn't already under contract for this film, I'd cut ties."

Three other women? And Vicky had planned on going in there, too? Reed Russell was the scourge of Hollywood. The sooner he was blacklisted, the better off the world would be. "Morals clause?"

"I'm not sure this is covered since they were caught *before* intercourse, but I'll be discussing it with the legal team prior to our meeting in the morning." Saul headed toward the stairs. "Get some sleep, Dante. I have a feeling tomorrow is going to be a long day."

Maybe, but to Dante it seemed like a weight had been lifted off his shoulders. Vicky was gone without any further interaction with Reed. She was safe from him, whether she knew it or not.

And the knowledge made Dante's heart beat a little steadier. Vicky might never realize it, but coming into his room instead of the one across the hall had saved her from the villain of this particular story. If he could find a way to make sure they *never* ended up together, maybe she'd cut him some slack for playing hero and rescuing her.

Chapter Three

Vicky texted as promised when she made it back to her apartment, then promptly stripped and fell into bed. It had been too long a day to do anything more. Her sleep was peppered with odd dreams she couldn't quite recall, but they woke her over and over, her heart racing and her sheets damp with sweat.

When sunlight seeped through the slits in her blinds and woke her fully, she rolled over with a groan. *I wish the monsters would stop chasing me or that the wild dream sex actually gave orgasms.*

As if summoned by the thought, her clit started to ache with need. Vicky groaned. This was what she got for going to the wrong room last night. No O, a body that sorely needed one—especially after seeing Dante…touching Dante—and a lunch date with Jade to get ready for. She slapped a hand on her nightstand until she found her phone to check the time. It was early enough. She could take care of business and still get cleaned up without getting to the restaurant late.

Thank goodness.

If Jade got even a hint that she was this needy, she'd wind up making back-room arrangements with the busboy. No thanks.

The drawer on her nightstand squealed as Vicky opened it. She'd have to oil the tracks later. Overuse was making them cranky.

"Hello, BOB, funny meeting you here again," she said to the purple vibrator in her hand. BOB, her battery-operated-boyfriend, was not nearly as good a substitute as she'd expected him to be. *All the fun, none of the drama.* Sure, she'd gotten a significant drama decrease, but *all* the fun was a big exaggeration. Not everything could be replaced by a machine. Or even a machine and a good imagination.

And Vicky had an *excellent* imagination.

It was one of the reasons she'd agreed to the deal with Jade in the first place. Only now she was paying for it in multiple ways. At least one of them she could take care of prior to lunch, though.

Closing her eyes, she let her hands skate down the swells and dips of her body, imagining it was him touching her. No name, no face. Just *him*. Her mystery man. Her muse. It could have been Reed. Or the cute guy at the bank. Or even the damn busboy. Here she didn't care. Here, they were all just BOB.

In her mind, the hands on her were bigger, rougher, scratchy against the softness of her skin. Friction like that made her want more touch. More pressure. She squeezed her nipples between her fingers, arching off the bed to the imaginary body above her.

He was naked, her mystery lover, and strong. He propped himself above her, his erection teasing, inches away from where she wanted it most.

Not wanted. Needed. She needed him.

Her hands left her nipples and glided down her body. Her right found the nub of her clit and started to rub as her other hand found her center. She slowly flicked those fingers at her opening like he would do with his tongue. Wetness seeped out, slicking her fingers as she imagined him going down on her, tasting her, feasting on her.

More. She needed more than this.

She imagined him crawling up her body as she grabbed BOB and turned on the vibration. Rubbing it against her clit, her lips, slipping ever so slightly into her opening, she could almost feel the tattooed man above her taking her breast in his mouth as he stroked into her at last.

She tilted her hips, giving herself access to that most sensitive spot inside. BOB hit it over and over again, pushing her higher and higher, keeping her on the crest of a wave she couldn't quite make it over.

The imaginary man lifted his head from her breast and smiled, sunlight catching in his brown eyes and making them twinkle as he said, "Bet you wish I'd left the piercing in, don't you?"

The orgasm tore through her with so much force, BOB was completely forgotten, yanked out as panic took hold. But even that couldn't overpower the strength of her release. She was still shaking by the time she grabbed the vibrator and shut it off.

Dante. Of all the people in the world…she'd imagined having sex with Dante Palladino. There were so many things wrong with that picture she wasn't sure she could count them all.

Brother's best friend.

The guy who'd almost broken up her engagement.

The one who had probably had more women than there'd been in her graduating class.

The one who likely saw her as nothing but a box on his bucket list. *Screw best friend's little sister. Check.*

The one she could have had just last night.

She could keep going, but she didn't need to. He was her brother's best friend, and the last guy she should be thinking about having sex with—ever. What she needed was a shower. She hadn't felt this dirty in forever.

And she didn't like how good it felt.

Not at all.

She made it to the café right on time. As usual, though, Jade was already there, flirting with the waiter. How her friend went so long between boyfriends Vicky had never figured out. Jade was the kind of woman who could find a guy anywhere and not only catch his attention but leave him lusting after her.

Vicky still remembered the time she'd left her purse at their table and had gone back to a restaurant just in time to hear the waiter and the bartender arguing over who had a better chance getting a date with her best friend…the friend who was already in her car and headed out of town.

She wished she had that sort of ability. Apparently Vicky gave off a fuck-you vibe instead of a flirtatious one. At least it was several steps up from the pathetic post-divorce funk she'd wallowed in for a while.

"Hey," she said as she approached the table.

Dismissing the waiter, Jade smiled up at her, then the grin shifted to something more contemplative. "You look different." Mouth dropping open slightly, she slapped her hand on the table. "You did it, didn't you? You got laid."

Vicky sat down on the vintage patio chair and scowled at her. "Could you keep it down a tiny bit? Not everyone needs to know about my sex life." Her shoulders slumped as she thought about last night, and worse, the aftermath that had been this morning. "Or lack thereof. BOB and I had a lovely time, though. Thanks for asking."

The frown aged Jade, making her look every one of her thirty years rather than the twenty-one she could normally pass for. "You're telling me there wasn't a single worthwhile guy at that party who tried to get in your pants? Or are you telling me you pussed out?"

"Does everything negative with you have to be compared to something female?"

"I'm not a misogynist. I'm a linguist. 'Pusillanimous' means lacking in courage."

"And to every normal person, it means pussy, as in vagina, as in female."

"Don't knock the vag—those things can take a pounding and come back for more." Jade waggled her eyebrows, breaking the weird tension of the moment.

"Pervert." Vicky laughed.

"Prude."

"In answer to your question, there was a guy. A hot guy. And then there was a comedy of errors that led to no sex.

No sex led to an interlude with BOB this morning that was its own kind of what-the-fuckery." Vicky sipped at the tea Jade had kindly ordered for her—chai rooibos, her favorite.

The waiter chose that moment to return, and they quickly put in their orders. The café had the best chicken salad sandwiches this side of the Pacific Ocean—possibly either side—they'd both known what they were getting without looking at the menu. "So, you're telling me there was a yummy man at the party who wanted to bang your bony ass… and you're here, having lunch with me?"

"First, my ass isn't bony."

"Yes, it is. Your badonkadonk was the first casualty of the divorce diet."

Where Jade embraced her size-ten curves and flaunted the hell out of them, Vicky had been a size four before Brandon left—with minimal curves—and she was almost back to that now. It was funny how she'd married the one guy who didn't fawn over her looks—initially it had been appealing, but over time it had become insulting. To the point that he'd compared her unfavorably to her friends. For a while after they split, she'd been borderline skeletal because of wallowing and not eating.

"Whatever. Point is, I missed my chance. Party's over. Today is meetings about some new movie." Vicky's phone buzzed in her purse, and she reached in to grab it, seeing a message from her boss about tomorrow's staff meeting. "And tomorrow is work…" When she went to stuff the phone away, she realized she wasn't having to stuff quite as much as normal. Frantic, she dug through the tiny bag.

"Your job sucks. You should come work for me instead."

"Yes, photographer to the stars, I'm sure I'd be a huge

asset as your…what, exactly?" It wasn't there. Where the hell…? *Shit.*

"You could be my oil girl—get the boys all nice and glossy for the shots." Jade paused as Vicky's shoulders slumped. "What's wrong?"

"Remember the comedy of errors?" At Jade's nod, she continued, "Apparently it isn't over. I knocked my purse off a table in his room and somehow missed picking up my work ID. It has my name, my picture…if someone returns it to Elegant and happens to mention it was found in a guest room, I'm so very fired."

"Sure you don't want the oil girl gig? I can't offer much in the way of real benefits, but there are a lot of hot men and the comedy stylings of yours truly on a daily basis."

She didn't want a job; she wanted a career. Elegant offered her that. It was a long road from entry-level waitress to party planner, but it was a good road. And if she blew it at Elegant, every company in the area would know why— she'd never get another shot. It'd be one menial job after another until she *maybe* found something else she was good at, something else she loved to do. "Jade…"

"Kidding. So, what do you think? Should we stage a break-in while they're deep in their meeting?"

Vicky knew her friend was joking, but at the moment it seemed like the best option they had. Especially considering the other one involved contacting Dante. She'd managed to mostly stay away from him last night like Evan had warned her to, but even their two brief exchanges had led to Dante-as-fantasy-guy this morning. Did she really want to risk seeing him again?

Did she have a choice?

Groaning, Vicky pulled her phone from her purse and started typing.

HEY. LEFT MY WORK BADGE IN YOUR ROOM. MORTENSEN MIGHT HAVE BEEN OKAY WITH ME STAYING LATE, BUT IF ANY OF THE STAFF FIND IT AND "HELP" BY TAKING IT TO ELEGANT, I'M FIRED.

It only took a few seconds before Dante sent his response.

FOUND IT THIS MORNING. HOW ABOUT I DROP IT BY YOUR PLACE TONIGHT AND WE CAN CATCH UP FOR REAL?

Considering she was terrified of what effect seeing him for even a few seconds would have on her libido, anything longer would end with her doing something stupid and having no choice but to take Jade's job offer. She'd never known anyone who affected her like Dante did. It was time to nip this in the bud before she lost control of the situation completely.

I'D REALLY FEEL BETTER ONCE IT'S BACK IN MY PURSE. I KNOW IT'S SILLY, BUT I'VE BEEN PARANOID ABOUT LOSING THIS JOB EVER SINCE I GOT IT. CAN I FLY BY THE MANSION AND PICK IT UP? I'M NOT FAR RIGHT NOW.

She expected him to argue, and when his response came, she was equal parts relieved and disappointed.

SURE THING. MEETING IS WRAPPING, AND I WAS GOING TO HEAD OUT FOR A RUN BEFORE I DISCUSS SOME STUFF WITH SAUL THIS AFTERNOON.

He'd given her an out. She'd better take it and count her lucky stars.

Perfect. See you in a few.

Vicky set the phone down and met Jade's quizzical expression. "Turns out the B and E isn't necessary. I just have to walk into my own personal level of hell instead. Want to come as backup?"

Jade set her coffee down and cocked her head sideways. "Now?"

"Yeah. I know, I know, I'm ditching you for a guy. Chicks before dicks and all that, but I need my job."

"You also need some dick, so I'd understand either way." Snorting, Jade snapped her fingers and the waiter came running like a trained dog. "We'll be taking our order to go. And cups for the drinks, too. Thanks." She turned back to Vicky and arched an eyebrow.

"I'm not going to get laid right now, Jade. I just want my badge."

"I know, sweetie. I was still hoping."

Maybe bringing her along was a bad idea. Jade was already like a dog with a bone in regard to Mission Re-pop Vicky's Cherry. Now, with the potential to close the deal within reach, she'd never let it go. Vicky had to try, though. "Do me a favor and stay in the car."

"I thought you wanted backup."

She had used that exact term, and Jade was a stickler for details when something had her attention. "I *might* need backup, but I'll wave you over if it comes to that. And if it does, please remember, this is about saving my job."

"Nope. Saving your job is just a bonus. As far as I'm concerned, this is still all about getting you a little something. Preferably a big something. Actually, I'm kind of hoping it's a Magnum-sized something."

She'd forgotten that Jade kept a condom selection to put most pharmacies to shame. "Can we please not go there right now?" Mainly because it had her thinking of a very specific penis—one that would need at least a Magnum.

"Well, expecting a Durex XXL guy might be pushing your luck." When Vicky shot her an angry glare, Jade just shrugged and said, "What? It would. Also, if that's what you're into, I should have bought you bigger toys."

They spent the rest of the drive in blessed silence. Now Jade was parked across the street from Mortensen's driveway, and Vicky was standing by the gate, waiting on Dante. She'd texted him the moment they'd arrived, but he hadn't come out yet. Loitering outside a Hollywood producer's mansion so hadn't been on today's to-do list. If a cop came by, she really had no good excuse. Saying she was meeting someone wouldn't go over well. As she was ready to text Jade for an assist, a man on foot came out the gate and started jogging down the sidewalk.

He tugged out earbuds and pulled off the stocking cap that had masked his long, dark hair when he stopped in front of her. "Hey, Vicks."

Two words and her insides were already turning to Jell-O. Time to do what she came for and get out of here. "Hey. So...do you have it?"

Dante chuckled. "You're making it sound like a drug deal is going down." He lowered his voice as he furtively pulled her badge from his pocket. When she went to grab it, he moved it out of reach. "But since we're dealing, I think that letting me take you to dinner tonight is a fair exchange for this little piece of plastic."

At the word "dinner," she made the mistake of looking at his mouth, and thoughts of his lips on hers—and on other, more sensitive bits of flesh—made heat coil inside her with need. She started to inch toward him without meaning to. No, just being near him was making her lose control, making her want to give herself to him. She had to stop this—right now—and there was only one way she could think to make that happen.

• • •

"Sorry. I already have plans with Reed tonight."

Had she not gotten the message last night? No. She hadn't been there when Saul had mentioned the other women.

"Did you miss me telling you he was bad news? The kind of guy who screws underage—" She laid a hand over his lips, and the touch was electrifying. The idea of her wasting that on fucking *Reed Russell* was infuriating.

"It doesn't matter. He asked. I said yes."

It *did* matter. She might have just been looking to get some post-divorce nookie, but Reed Russell was *not* the guy to do it with. There was no way he was leaving her alone with that kind of danger. Somehow, Dante had to put the brakes on this. If he didn't, and Evan found out he could have… Well, he didn't want to be involved in that kind of conversation. But clearly, Vicky wasn't interested in the truth, at least not right now. That would just lead to her arguing and leaving, more determined than ever to meet up with Reed and attempt to prove him wrong.

Which meant, as much as he hated it, Dante had to play this the way Reed would. Which involved doing something so ugly his lunch threatened to come back up. "You know, it wouldn't take much for me to tell the whole truth about last night."

Vicky's eyes widened as she stared at him. "What?"

"You left this in my room." He waved her badge up over her head. "Same room you were in minus your panties and wearing a gorgeous lacy bra. I wonder how your boss would like hearing about that when I drop this by his office." She stopped leaping for the badge, and he caught her gaze again. "Or you could cancel on Reed and go to dinner with me instead."

"You're blackmailing me?" The words came from between teeth clenched tight. "To date you?"

To date…?

He'd been thinking to blackmail her just to stay the hell away from Reed and the kind of trouble he represented, and he'd hoped one night would do that. But could he really pass up a chance to let Vicky get to know him? After all this time? That window of opportunity he'd recognized the night before opened wider, displaying a view filled with all sorts of chasms and dangers. It wasn't a pretty one, but if it kept her out of Reed's clutches, it was still the right choice to make.

"Something like that."

Fury and panic warred on her face, painting it in reds and tight lines. She grabbed his arm, but when he didn't drop the badge, she stood on her tiptoes and whispered in his ear, her voice heartbroken more than angry, "Since it seems what I heard five years ago was right, I'd rather lose my job."

Ouch. Regardless of what she'd heard about him, it still wasn't enough to convince Dante to hand her over to the guy who would happily destroy more than just her new career. "Good to know. I guess my run can wait until later." He turned as if to go back through the gate.

Her fingers tightened on his biceps, holding him in place, and her face screwed up in a mask of frustration and anger. "Why do you have to be such an ass?"

"What can I say, Vicks? You bring out the best in me." He laid a hand over hers, ready to peel back her fingers one at a time to really drive home the illusion that he planned to run and tattle on her. "So, dinner tonight, or am I going inside to ask Saul the name of the guy at Elegant?"

She twisted around as if looking for an escape, then let out a furious screech as a tour bus rumbled slowly past. "Just dinner?"

"Dinner tonight and you get your badge back. A few more nights out over the next couple weeks and you have my word that no one will know about the little birthmark on your left ass cheek."

A blush crept up her skin as she cast a glance toward the gate, then another toward the road. Whatever she was looking for must not have been there. She bit her lip in a way that made him want to pull it free. "You're not exactly leaving me much choice."

Saul was in the process of firing Reed from the movie as they spoke, so it wasn't likely Vicky would run into him any time soon. As long as he kept her away tonight, she'd probably be safe. "It's just dinner, Vicky."

"And a couple more nights."

"Let's just worry about tonight. Badge back, and then

your boss would have to make you strip down to prove I'm not a lying son of a bitch anyway."

She snorted a laugh and shook her head. "I forgot about your way with words. Fine. I'll do it."

"That way with words is called honesty. And so is this." Emboldened by their ridiculous deal, he leaned in and pressed his mouth to hers. He didn't know what he expected, but having his whole body light on fire sure as hell wasn't it. She'd been in his bed just last night, and it hadn't felt this intense. For a split second, her lips softened beneath his, as if she felt it, too, and was surrendering to the energy flowing between them.

Then she stiffened again.

Any fleeting hope that she'd felt something deep and real vanished. Post-divorce kiss, he'd seen it before—the need for connection so intense that in the right moment anything would suffice. He was going to have to do better than that with Vicky if he wanted this to last beyond the ruse, beyond the moment when he admitted the blackmail itself was the lie.

For now, he simply drew back from the kiss and combed his fingers through her hair. "I'll call you about dinner in a couple hours."

Then he stuffed her badge in his pocket, yanked on his cap, and took off at a jog. Earbuds back in place, he almost laughed at the song that had shuffled onto his warm-up mix, wondering if his old friend Lee had reached down from the afterlife to voice his opinion on the matter. The chorus of "If That's What It Takes" by Bon Jovi summed up the last ten minutes of his life. As his feet slapped the concrete, he found himself humming along. Maybe by the time their two weeks were up, Vicky would understand his intentions, too.

Chapter Four

Vicky's ass hadn't touched the leather seat before Jade said, "Are you kidding me?"

"What?" As soon as Vicky shut the door, Jade was pulling from the curb and executing a tight U-turn.

"You almost hooked up with the Inferno? And you failed to mention that part? I swear, that kind of omission makes me question our friendship."

The Inferno. Dante's nickname from his pro wrestling days. He'd been one of the "good guys"—the entire shtick around his character was that he'd been sent from hell to punish evildoers and make them turn from the wickedness of their ways. He'd rocked the guyliner and a thick bloodred streak in his hair. He still used the look for certain events... and it still made Vicky's panties wet. She'd never let anyone know, though, especially not her brother. Or Dante.

"It's not nearly that simple. And he's mainly acting now. He's kind of ditched the nickname."

Jade cast side-eyes at her. "Only you could complicate sex with a man like that."

"We haven't had sex, so it's not complicated…yet. It's just not as simple as you like to make everything." When Jade only snorted in response, Vicky continued, "He's Evan's best friend, *and* before I married Brandon, my brother told me Dante was bad news." *His blackmailing me with my damn badge kind of proves it. And to think, I'd been all worried about how I'd give in to him and lose myself in a relationship again.*

"Meh. Unless he tests positive for something icky, I can't imagine how a little bump and grind with him could be bad." Pausing at a red light, she tapped her nails on the steering wheel. "Unless he has a micropenis. That could be bad."

As if Jade's words had conjured a phantom dick into the car, Vicky could feel his thickness and length in her hand again. Her insides tightened around nothing, complaining about the sexual release she'd been denied. "He doesn't."

"How close are they that Evan knows that?" Jade laughed. When Vicky didn't join in, she cocked her head to the side. "Your brother never would have brought that up. *You* know it. How close to sex did you get?"

"Close enough I know how big his dick is, and that's probably as close as I should get." The light turned green, and Vicky prayed Jade would let it go.

"Uh-uh, sugar. You have a timeline, and based on what I saw, that was a man who would be more than happy to help you prove me wrong by showing both of us that you *can* do just sex. Stick it to me while he sticks it in you." A horn blasted behind them, and Jade shoved her hand out the window, flashing him the bird, but she did pull back into traffic.

Vicky wished she could sink into the leather and disappear. This entire situation had spiraled out of control. "Rushing into something with him just seems like a colossally bad idea. I mean, if Evan of all people warned me off, shouldn't I take that as solid advice?" Besides, she could already feel herself getting lured in. It wouldn't be just sex—not to her.

"Yes. And you did. Before you got married. Times change, people change, and it's not like you're looking for a forever romance here. You're just trying to get a good, solid, not-mechanically-induced orgasm. Maybe even a couple. You need it, and you deserve it. And really, you could do a lot worse than the Inferno. There are women who would literally kill to be in your position."

"I told you," she said, sinking a little lower, "he doesn't like people using that name anymore." *And neither do I. I don't need reminders of how hot he is—it's been branded in my head for years.*

• • •

Dante needed a plan.

Saul hadn't fired Reed after all. The little asshole's lawyer had argued the "indiscretion" had happened at a private party and none of the women involved were upset about anything other than the interruption. Due to that, the lawyer helpfully mentioned an announcement of Reed's termination would have to be followed with a statement from the actor, which would include spilling the details about where the incident had taken place.

In the end, Saul had caved. The film didn't need any more bad press. They'd already had to recast the female lead due to their first choice landing in rehab after a particularly violent drug-induced episode that left her boyfriend in the hospital.

Bad enough they had to put up with Reed and his shit on set. This also meant that he'd be around for every event Dante had hoped to attend with Vicky. If it were an option, he'd just bail and take her somewhere else—anywhere else—but the only ones that weren't contractually obligated were charity events, and he wasn't about to skip those.

On the plus side, he had a couple days to figure it out before they needed to deal with Reed—if she stuck around that long. And soon, he'd have Vicky all to himself at dinner. She'd insisted on driving separately, but a lot of women did that these days. He'd hoped to avoid the potential-creeper label based on his friendship with Evan, and the fact that she'd known him for several years, but he wasn't about to give her grief about being cautious.

He only wished she had applied the same logic to her interaction with Reed.

Late evening sun beat down on the concrete, blasting the last of the day's heat like a furnace. He could have waited inside, but a stupid part of him relished the idea of taking Vicky's arm as the valet held her car door open.

"Are we waiting for sunset or something?"

Her voice would have made him jump if Lee hadn't trained him to not react to unexpected sounds. "Where did you come from?"

Turning, he drank her in. Gone were the miniskirt and white blouse. Gone, too, were the shorts and T-shirt from earlier. In their place, she wore a flowy dark peach dress. It was long in the back, but shorter in the front to show off her amazing legs. He couldn't have picked a more perfect outfit to accentuate her coloring and body. She was, in a word, stunning.

"I parked down the street. I can't afford valet parking. Waitress, remember?"

"I would have covered it for you."

"And I don't need you to come to my rescue. I'm a big girl who can handle a couple blocks in heels." She swept the hair off her shoulders and tipped her head toward the door. "So, are you planning to feed me or are we taking over for the valet? Regardless of the walk I mentioned, if it's the latter, I would have worn different shoes."

"Definitely not the latter. The shoes look too good on you to get rid of." They did, too. The nude leather matched her skin, and the stiletto heels made her legs look a mile long. He rested his hand on the small of her back and led her to the door. "You look gorgeous, by the way."

She arched a brow, just a slight raise, as if she wasn't amused enough to give him the full depth of her sarcasm, but he also saw the flush of pleasure rising in her cheeks at the compliment. "Were you expecting me to show up in a burlap sack?"

"Never that," he said as the maître d' led them to their table. "I guess I wasn't sure if you cared enough to dress up." He pulled a chair out for her and caught the very obvious roll of her eyes.

"Even if you were the most hated man in America, I would have respected the restaurant enough to dress appropriately."

He didn't know why, but the way she was acting... Vicky was *trying* to keep her distance, as if she didn't want to let herself get too close, lest she get burned. Was he never going to lose that damn nickname? At least she was still talking. That was something, right? Dante took his seat across from her and glanced at the wine menu. "Do you have a preference?"

"To be snuggled up with a good book."

Or not.

He handed the wine list to the maître d'. "Bring us your top recommendation." As soon as the man was out of earshot, Dante leaned across the table. "You always could have stood me up if you really didn't want to be here."

"Give up a free dinner for the privilege of having you tell my boss I tried to seduce you? No, thanks."

Right. The blackmail, and the likely reason she was being so pissy. What the hell had he ever done to make her believe he'd actually stoop that low? Sure, he'd threatened it to get her away from Reed, but that was as far as he'd go. Had she told him to shove it up his ass, he would have let the whole plot dissolve. Maybe talked to Evan about her plans and had him deal with it, but he *never* would have said a word to her boss. "About that…"

"Let it go, Dante. I'm here. Let's just eat, and you can tell me what other things I'm required to attend with you." She slid a piece of paper across the table at him. "My work schedule, since I'm sure you didn't take that into account."

He definitely hadn't. Even the days she finished work early, he'd be taking her out after she'd been on her feet all day. It made him feel like a first-class jackass. That was the moment the plan he needed to pull together shifted from individual threads into a perfectly knit blanket, one that would cover her work worries and give her a break from her job.

His lips twitched toward a smile he couldn't show her, and he had to school it to something more serious as he pushed the paper back toward her. "You're right. I didn't account for that. But if your boss knows you have an in with your brother's old friend who happens to be looking to throw a big party to celebrate both their birthdays next month… maybe he'll be willing to cut back your waitressing hours in order to let you take charge of the account."

"Right. From waitress to party planner overnight? You realize that my five-year plan had party planner at the end of it—and I'd have been happy enough with *assistant* tacked on to the front of that title. So, I'd ask what you were on, but you *are* the guy who's all about clean living." The way she said it made it clear she didn't believe a word she heard about him, either.

"I'm not on anything. What's the office number again?" He pulled his phone from his pocket.

"Stop it. You aren't funny."

When she wasn't forthcoming, he did a quick search for Elegant Entertainment, pulled up the number, and hit call. Voicemail picked up on the first ring, and Vicky's eyes went wide as he spoke. "Hi, Mr. Collins, this is Dante Palladino. We met at Saul's party last night. My best friend's birthday is the same month as mine, and I ran into his younger sister there last night, too. I'd really like her to plan a party at my home. I know she's currently in your employ, so if you could clear her calendar for the next couple weeks, I'd be happy to come to your office and sign a contract for this. If it causes any unforeseen expenses on your part, we can discuss compensation for that as well." He left his number and then ended the call, sliding her badge across the table at the same time.

The expression of abject shock on Vicky's face made the cost of a party well worth it. She shook her head slowly, her eyes narrowing. "Why are you doing this?"

"Getting you a better job? A few reasons. First, it'll give you a shot you would have waited months, if not years, for otherwise. Second, for at least a couple weeks, you'll make more money. Third, your schedule is a lot more flexible now. That last one's a bit selfish, I admit." Hero to the rescue again.

"I don't need you to hand me a promotion." Vicky sat silently for a moment as their wine was served, her eyes never leaving his. Slowly, as he sampled the wine, her glare faded to something softer, kinder. "But thank you."

When the wine steward left, Dante allowed himself to smile at her. "Vicks, I didn't give you a promotion. I gave you a shot at one. This won't be a bullshit job. You need to plan a party, and your boss has to be impressed. The only difference is your first client wants you to succeed as much as you do."

"I…" She bit her lip and stared into the depths of her wine, swirling it in the glass. "I told you before, you don't need to save me. But I do really appreciate this."

"Like I said, it's more than a little selfish on my part." He reached across the table and rested his hand on hers, stilling the movement of her glass. "In the meantime, I promised to feed you. Let's figure out dinner."

• • •

Vicky dreamed of Dante again and woke cursing his name.

Why did he have to be so freaking beautiful? And why the hell was he helping her? This wasn't the bad news her brother had warned her about. Instead he was doing all the right things, going above and beyond the call of a first date. And it was driving her batty.

After dinner, he'd walked her to her car, insisting he'd be the worst date ever if he let her go alone. It was just like the night before—only this time she was with him because he'd forced her to be rather than because she'd sneaked into the wrong damn bed. She'd expected him to get pushy once they arrived at her Acura, insist the night wasn't over. But not only had he not suggested they should go back to his place, he hadn't even gone in for a good-night kiss.

This morning, her lips still ached, yearning for something she hadn't gotten. Something she shouldn't have even wanted.

In the dream, he'd leaned in close, more than once, his mouth so near hers there was barely space for breath between them. But it had never progressed beyond that, almost as if her own brain were admonishing her for not kissing *him* after dinner.

She wanted to scream her frustration to the wind.

Instead, she settled for scrubbing herself viciously in the shower. *I'll just loofah him right out of my head.* Too bad it only reminded her of all the places he'd never touched her.

Not him. He's *not supposed to touch me anywhere.*

These two weeks were going to kill her.

The drive to work was long, and she spent it trying to come up with explanations in case Mathew asked her what the hell she was doing with Dante. Worse, if Mathew talked to Saul Mortensen, he might have caught wind of her late-night visit. Even worse, Dante himself might have decided to spill since she *hadn't* moved in for a kiss or something more last night.

So many scenarios, so little time.

She still had a dozen possibilities racing through her head when she walked through the door. And then time for concocting responses ended as Mathew stepped from the shadow of the reception desk and said, "Ms. Stone, can I see you in my office?"

"Of course. Did you want me to clock in first?"

"That won't be necessary."

Oh, that didn't sound good. She followed him down the hall, accompanied by the stares of far too many coworkers. Obviously this wasn't a normal occurrence to people who had been around awhile.

Mathew's office was as stark as she'd remembered. He'd told her that he preferred it that way because it kept potential clients from seeing any specific theme or style he might press on them for their events. His office was a blank canvas, as every party plan would be. At the moment, however, it was oppressive. Kind of the way she imagined an empty prison cell would be as you walked through the door.

"Have a seat." Mathew waved a long-fingered hand toward one of the straight-backed chairs in front of his desk.

Vicky gave one yearning glance at the sitting area behind her before taking her spot in the horribly uncomfortable metal chair. This obviously wasn't a social meeting.

He steepled his fingers and stared at her long enough that she started sweating and had to fight the urge to fidget. She hadn't done anything wrong. Well, not really. Sure she'd *planned* to have sex with a party guest. And she *had* ended up in another guest's bed, where she'd put her hand on his rock-hard, pierced cock. But…

Great. Now I'm getting turned on. I'm going to kill Dante.

"I got an interesting message this morning from Dante Palladino."

Okay. Interesting didn't mean bad, and probably only referred to the message she'd heard him leaving last night. Best to play it off like it was news to her. "Oh?"

"It seems you two have a history."

Old history or recent history? How much did Mathew know? "He and Evan have been best friends for years. And we ran into each other Saturday night, as you saw. Again, sorry for lingering as long as I did with him. Every time I went to walk away, he would decide he wanted more crostini." She shrugged, brushing it off as actor craziness.

Mathew tapped his fingers on the desk, the beats far too similar to the sound of a death march. "The call wasn't about that, exactly." The drumming stopped, and Vicky waited for him to drop the ax. "He wants you to plan a birthday party for himself and your brother."

That was it? She let out a sigh and tried not to let the relief show on her face. "I'd love to."

"I'm sure you would. So would several people who have been with Elegant Entertainment years longer than you. However, I spoke to Mr. Palladino already, and he was quite insistent. It was either you or he'd look into other options. Any idea why he'd be so determined?" The drumming started again, slower this time.

Because he wants me to be at his beck and call? "It's probably because he knows my situation. I'm making a new life start, and this is his way of helping out. Of course, it's also beneficial to the planning that I know the likes and dislikes of both the client and the other birthday boy." Mathew's eyes narrowed, and Vicky started to get pissed. Sure, what Dante was doing was a little underhanded, but she did have experience. She'd planned more than one of Evan's parties over the years—the only difference between then and now was she had a boss calling the shots these days. Which meant she could always give him something to consider. "Honestly, if he's talking about looking into other options, there's a good chance Dante will just call me directly. This party can either be mutually beneficial, or I can use it to make money on the side. I suppose that's up to you."

His fingers stopped tapping on the desk, the pause abrupt and jarring. For a long moment his hand stayed in that position, as if she'd frozen time, then he laid it flat on the desktop. "And what would you expect from an opportunity like this?"

Hot damn, he was on the hook. "For starters, complete creative control once a budget is worked out. Obviously I'd need access to staff and supplier lists, as well as awareness of any standard up-charges so I know what I really have to work with as well as where I can get the best deals. I also need to know if I'm permitted to move outside that network if I deem it necessary to make the client happy."

"Complete creative control and access to supply chain? If I didn't know better, I'd be worried you planned to strike out on your own and arranged this whole thing so you would have insider info on how to be most competitive."

Mathew narrowed his eyes at her, but Vicky's only response was to laugh. "You know my situation as well, if not better, than Dante does. I don't have the means to start my own business, and you know damn well I won't take money from my brother to do it. If that was my goal, Dante never would have come to you with the offer in the first place, he'd have just hired me straight out." Instead of returning his glare, she cocked her head to the side and favored her boss with a tight smile. "Oh, a couple more things—I expect to have the rest of my schedule cleared in order to give this party the attention it requires, and I expect to be paid what any other planner would be for an event similar in scope and attendance. Of course, ultimately, the decision is yours."

Chapter Five

When Dante had gotten the call to set up a meeting this afternoon, he'd texted Vicky immediately.

Looks like congratulations are in order. Does this mean we can have our first planning session tonight?

It took less than a minute to get a reply.

Make sure you let Mathew know you want that. I get paid overtime if I work past five.

He rubbed at the scruff on his face, his hand effectively covering his smile. It wasn't a no. It wasn't even a *why don't we meet after you sign the contract?* Maybe she was starting to actually enjoy spending time with him.

What if he says no?

It was possible, after all. Even though Dante planned to include "odd hours" in the contract to ensure they were able to spend time together…as well as her getting paid.

WE'LL FIGURE IT OUT THEN, I GUESS.

And that had been a little too noncommittal for his taste. When it came time for his meeting with Mathew, Dante decided to play hardball. He wanted Vicky on retainer until the party happened. The man balked and tried to force him into a more modest option, but Dante didn't want any part of that.

"Mr. Collins… May I call you Mathew? Well, Mathew, you see, filming starts on my new movie soon, and I'm going to have to do all my planning with Vicky between takes and at odd hours. It would be the same no matter who I hired, but it's likely she'll make better use of her time based on simple knowledge of myself and her brother. But I really need her on my schedule, not some nine-to-five crap."

Mathew swept a hand through his blond hair. It looked like a toupee, but Dante wasn't about to call the guy out on it. It didn't matter if women had jumped on the bald-is-beautiful bandwagon; the guy already had his short stature working against him in life. If Mathew Collins thought he needed the hair, he could have the hair without comment from Dante.

"Mr. Palladino…"

"Dante, please." He smiled, showing off his nearly per-fect teeth. His agent had once said that Helen might have had the face that launched a thousand ships, but Dante had the smile that could draw them all off course.

"Dante." Collins slid a sheet of paper across his desk. "This is what you're looking at costwise for nothing but the planning, and that only allows for ten hours a week overtime in Vicky's pay. She's going to have to sign off on it as well, since you can't guarantee you won't need her more off hours than that."

Shrugging, Dante shoved the paper back. "As long as she's game, I'm in, but it will be in the contract that she handles this account. I don't want it passed off to someone else because you decide you need her as a waitress."

"I understand. You want to make sure she's given a fair shot." Collins smoothed down his tie. "What you're doing for your friend's sister is admirable, even if I think there are people better suited to the job. I hope the two of you prove me wrong." He pushed a button on his phone. "Stone, my office, please."

"Right away." Vicky's voice was lighter than Dante had heard it since…well, since before she was married. Definitely lighter than the past couple days.

Collins nodded to him. "I'm assuming you have at least a little time to draw up a rough proposal with her now?"

"Of course. It's why I wanted to get started immediately." That and getting her off the outrageous work schedule. As soon as the door opened, he stood, turning to smile at her. "Sounds like we can get to work as soon as you approve the schedule."

Vicky nodded. "Sure thing. I'm guessing there's not a lot of wiggle room with it, anyway." She gave Mathew a pointed glance, and the man squirmed.

"Even considering Dante's request for late work hours, I think it's more than fair." He handed over the paper.

Giving a shrug, Vicky nodded. "I suppose it is. I'm just wondering how you want me to track my hours. I'm not exactly going to drive into the office to clock in and out before I meet him on set—or wherever it is he needs me. I mean, most planners are salary instead of hourly, so it's not an issue, but in this case…"

She let the question dangle, and Mathew started to squirm more. "I trust you to report your hours for this on the honor system. Just keep track of when you start and stop working."

"What about working through lunch and that?"

He let out a sigh. "Report your time to the nearest quarter hour daily. Is that reasonable?"

"Totally." She grabbed a pen from his desktop, scribbled a note on the paper, and shoved it toward him. "Added that bit, and now it's all signed. If you can just initial the change or something. Do you need Dante's John Hancock, too?"

Clearly her boss hadn't expected her to be smart enough to get that in writing, because he paled slightly as he signed the paper. "No. Mr. Palladino's signature"—*oh, it's Mr. Palladino again now?*—"on the contract will be fine. I'll email it to you with the max estimate of your fees included. You have everything else you need?"

"Yep. Your secretary has been really helpful. We'll have the contract signed and back by the end of the day." Vicky opened the door, holding it wide. "After you, *Mr. Palladino*."

Vicky practically danced out of Mathew's office. Her earlier ambivalence about the party was obviously gone. She must not have been irritated that Dante had set it up—not after she'd seen how much more she could make in the few weeks she'd act as his party planner.

"You're looking pretty chipper." Dante eased past her into what appeared to be a temporary office: bookshelves with nothing but a few binders, a desk with no personal items, and mismatched chairs that had probably been shoved in here this morning. He swiped a finger along one of the shelves. "Wow. Could he have given you a worse office?"

"Until about an hour ago, I didn't *have* an office. I'm not going to bitch." She sat on the far side of the desk and flipped open a laptop. "Ready to get to work?"

He contemplated the chair across from her, but he didn't have high hopes that it was any sturdier than it looked. "Ready for you to print out whatever you absolutely must have on hand for us to talk. That way we can get some lunch."

"Lunch?"

Smiling, Dante leaned forward, hands on her desk, and caught her gaze. "Yeah. Lunch. I'm hungry. Aren't you hungry, Vicks?"

Her breathing changed, slightly quicker and deeper, making her breasts heave beneath the fitted button-down. She ran a tongue over her lips and swallowed. "Sure."

"Fantastic." He shoved away from the desk, putting distance between them before he took her body's unintentional cues as an invitation to do something he shouldn't. "I know a great place just down the road."

Vicky blinked at him rapidly as if snapping out of a daydream. "It'll just take a second to print this stuff."

Minutes later, they were seated across from each other at a little diner. It was like they'd stepped right into a fifties teen movie set, from the black-and-white tiled floor and red vinyl benches right down to the waitresses' fitted pinup-style uniforms. Neon lights overhead made everything seem more surreal.

Glancing around as she opened her menu, Vicky said, "This is a bit of a change from last night."

"This is more me than last night." Dante nodded to the waitress. He'd been coming here since he first moved to L.A., the only difference between then and now were some of the staff and the size tips he could afford to leave. "Try the Diner Fries, they're amazing."

"Diner Fries? Like…French fries?"

"The owners met in Montreal and lived there for years. Diner Fries are their version of poutine—fries with gravy and cheese."

"Fantastic. I can feel my arteries hardening already." Vicky put down the menu. "So, about the party…"

Before he could answer, a waitress stepped up to them. "Dante, I haven't seen you in a while. Want me to put the fries in now?"

"Hey, Dolores, this is Vicky, and she's afraid the fries will kill her." He winked at the woman.

She flipped a long, white ponytail over her shoulder and said, "Young lady, I am seventy-two years old, and I've been splurging on those fries at least once a week since I was a teenager. I can't guarantee you'll be active at my age, but I can promise you trying the fries won't be the thing that keeps it from happening."

Vicky's face was crinkled in a mask of mortification. "I guess we need fries, then. And water. May I please have a glass of water?"

"Water and Diner Fries coming up. You want anything else right now?"

"No, just water for me, too. We'll be here awhile if you

don't mind, though." Dante waved toward the binder next to Vicky.

Dolores winked at him and bounced away, saying, "You're one of my favorite customers. You can stay as long as you like."

The instant she was behind the counter, Vicky whispered, "She's *seventy-two*?"

"Still acts like a teenager with her husband, too." Dante laughed. "He was an American attending college in Canada. She was the daughter of some local bigwig. Their relationship caused a huge uproar in her family. Turned into a total forbidden love thing, complete with the sneaking out and the threats against his life. When he graduated, they ran away together, got married, and settled here. Very *Romeo and Juliet*, but with a much happier ending."

She craned her neck to the side, as if trying to watch Dolores. A faraway look haunted her eyes. "And her family?"

"Let's just say grandchildren can have an incredible effect at bridging a divide. Her mother came around first, eventually forcing everyone else to see just how happy Dolores and Mark were together. After that, her parents came to visit every year for the holidays until they passed away."

Vicky shook her head, as if scattering thoughts. "How do you know all this? *Why* do you know all this about them?"

"Because I asked? I like to know about people." He stopped talking as Dolores delivered their water and fries. They spent a minute giving the rest of their order, then he returned to the question. As true as his answer was, it hadn't been the whole truth, and maybe it was time he shared that with someone. "Thing is, when I left wrestling, I came out here with nothing but a name and a prayer. No acting lessons, no skills, really. Sure, I had some money, but I didn't know what to do with myself. Then I found this place."

"And there happened to be a big director sitting at this very table who took one look at you and had to cast you in something?" Vicky picked up a fry, twisting it in the cheese and gravy in a way designed to wipe it all off but only managing to get more stuck.

"Hardly. The waitress who took my order went into labor and—"

"And you jumped to the rescue and delivered the baby with the aid of a kitchen knife and a bendy straw."

This time Dante laughed, loud and long. He'd been so far from a hero then; he'd been a mess. "*I* panicked. Dolores jumped in like she'd been on hand for a hundred babies being born, and all I could do was sit and watch. When the ambulance got here to take the waitress to the hospital, Dolores muttered something about being shorthanded and wondering who was going to do the damn dishes. My very first job in Hollywood was washing dishes in that kitchen." He pointed toward the food window behind the counter.

"I never knew you did grunt work after you came here."

"Because I never saw it that way. On the day I started, I saw it as stepping up where I'd failed to with the waitress. After that…" He thought back to long days with Dolores and her family, finding his place in this crazy new world. "Let's just say working here made it possible for me to not lose myself in the Hollywood machine. This diner made me humble. It made me human. It made me the guy you know."

• • •

Vicky popped the fry in her mouth, chewing on both the potato and his words. Before she realized what she was doing, she reached for another. Okay, maybe they were as good as he'd said, but the rest of it? She didn't know him, not really. Once upon a time, she'd thought she had, but Evan had told her she was wrong. And with him blackmailing her and then helping her get a shot at work, she was even more confused. Who was Dante really? Hero or heartbreaker? And with the promise to herself not to get involved with a man until she had her own shit together—did she really want to know? She didn't have the strength to keep herself whole and be with him, not yet.

"I think…" When she looked at him, she saw the same thing in his eyes she'd seen years ago—a fire that made her yearn for warmth. She saw a guy who had an indefinable *something* she'd never seen in her life before or since. But no matter how much she wanted to find out what it was, she couldn't help remembering Evan's warning: *When you play with fire, sometimes you get burned.* Her body, which had gone on some sort of sexually charged alert while Dante was talking, deflated. "I think you were right about the fries. Totally worth the artery damage."

When he looked at her now, the blaze dimmed, not to a sexy smolder, but to little more than an ember. It didn't matter that he still smiled at her. She'd doused whatever had been flaring between them. "Glad you like them. Now, about the party, I'm guessing probably between fifty and a hundred people."

It took her a full thirty seconds to register that he'd taken her let's-change-the-subject and run with it. "Um. Yeah. We might need to narrow it down a bit, but we can start there.

Were you thinking of renting a place?"

"I was hoping to have it at my house."

She hadn't really considered it, but between the wrestling money and the movie money, Dante's house was probably more than big enough. "What kind of square footage are we talking?"

He shrugged, like it didn't matter. "The house is about seven thousand square feet, but the yard is huge, too. I was thinking we could do tents outside, have it be a little more casual."

Seven thousand square feet. Did he even know what that sounded like compared to her little one-bedroom apartment? On the other hand, it really wasn't fair to bitch. Evan would have set her up somewhere nice if she'd let him, but she hadn't. She needed to do this on her own, and that meant starting from the ground up. And no one started with seven thousand square feet of ground. "Casual works. Did you give any thought to theme? Regardless of what you told Mathew, I haven't exactly spent much time with you and Evan the last few years."

"You're telling me you don't know your brother?"

No. Of course she knew him. She could plan a party for *him* in a heartbeat. Vicky bit her lip, abandoned the fries, and cast a glance out the window. "I don't know *you.*"

Slowly, like he was afraid she'd bolt if he moved too fast, he reached across the table and took her hand in his. "How about we change that?"

Vicky couldn't look away from their fingers twined together. The touch was so innocent, so sweet... Could he *really* be the guy Evan had warned her about? And damn it, should she be judging him based on a warning five years old? Much less her own fears about men? "What did you have in mind?"

"I was thinking some time together that isn't all business." His thumb rubbed circles on the top of her hand.

No pressure, just enough contact to remind her he was there. Maybe hint that he wasn't going anywhere if she wanted him to stay. As an offer, it was terrifying. She couldn't trust that he'd stick around—that any guy would stick around. But part of her—the part that hadn't died with her marriage—wanted to let herself believe. It wasn't like he was promising her happily ever after. This wasn't love—it was friendship. Sexually charged friendship, but friendship nonetheless. She could handle things as long as she kept that in mind. "Not all business could be nice."

Chapter Six

Dante lowered the bar onto the cradle before he hurt himself. He was going to drive himself nuts if he couldn't stop thinking about Vicky. At the moment, he seemed incapable of even making it through a damn workout without her invading his mind.

"You okay, man?" Tony, his spotter, frowned down at him.

"Yeah. Just a lot on my mind."

"Good thing I'm here or you would have had about three fifteen on your chest." Tony laughed.

Dante had a hard time sharing his humor, though. "And I appreciate it. I think I'm done for today. I need to go to a meeting anyway." He sat up and slapped Tony on the shoulder before standing and heading to the shower.

He didn't want to think about the damage he could have done if he'd dropped that kind of weight on himself. The shower pounded against tile as he stripped. When he'd pictured spending all this time with Vicky, he hadn't really taken into account how much he'd want to touch her. Even at the diner yesterday, it had been all he could do to keep the contact innocent. And now? She was filling every fucking moment, whether she was present or not.

What had he been thinking? He knew damn well how often he'd fantasized about having Vicky in his bed. And his car. And his...everywhere. He'd spent five years feeling guilty over even thinking about his best friend's sister like that, and now he was going to have her practically at his beck and call. It would be great, if not for the constant reminder that the moment she'd found herself in bed with him, she'd freaked.

He could almost hear Lee's voice in his head, admonishing him for his stupidity. *If the answer's no, the answer's no. You're never going to change it. Better to look for a different question.*

The more he thought about it, the more he wondered *why* she'd freaked so much. Sure, being in the wrong guy's bed was embarrassing, but it wasn't like they were strangers. If anything, Dante was probably her best wrong-bed scenario. He wasn't the guy to trap her in his room and demand she finish what she started. Or report her to anyone—regardless of what he'd threatened.

He was the one who'd helped sneak her out of the house, for fuck's sake.

No. It wasn't a simple thing. There was something deeper going on with her than embarrassment over having her hand on his cock. Now he just had to figure out how to ask the question without pushing her away.

His phone was ringing when he twisted off the water,

and he snatched it from the bench before the call went to voicemail. "Dante."

"Hey, I'm going to have to postpone our meeting."

Vicky, and she was blowing him off already. So much for getting answers. "For how long?"

"Uh…I don't know? I have a massive leak under my sink, and the super isn't answering his phone. I'd just let it go, but I'm not sure who's responsible if it damages anything in here or the apartment below mine."

"Let me guess, the plumber gave you something like a four-hour window for when he's going to show." Even if it wasn't just a line, which it very well might've been, that put them at sharing dinner…again, rather than spending the day together.

Vicky barked a laugh. "Are you kidding? It'd be at least a hundred dollars just to have someone come out and look. If I can't fix it myself, I'll throw a bucket under there and hope my super gets here before things get out of control."

Which meant she wasn't really canceling, only delaying like she'd said. "How much experience do you have with plumbing?"

"Aside from my own?" She paused, but not long enough for him to actually respond to the joke. "It'll be fine. I mean, how much damage can I really do? It's already leaking."

She was going to flood the entire building. He could see it now. "I'll be over as quickly as I can."

"That's not necessary. I'll give you a call as soon as I know when I can meet up with you." And then she hung up on him.

Shit. Still wet from the shower, he yanked his clothes on, grabbed his stuff, and was out the door. Ideally, he would have had time to run back to his place and grab tools, but he only hoped Vicky had whatever was needed to get the job done.

Plus, if he managed to swoop in and save the day, maybe it would be a window toward getting some of those answers he was hoping for. He was just glad he'd made a point of sharing addresses at the diner, since odds were they'd need them during party planning anyway, otherwise he would have had to waste precious minutes tracking her down. All things considered, he made good time getting to Vicky's place. Even so, when he got to her apartment door, he was met with a high-pitched screech followed by a stream of cursing that would have made a sailor proud.

Dante pounded on the door. "Vicky?"

She yelled from inside, "It's about damn time! The door's unlocked."

And here he'd wondered if she was going to be upset about him showing up after she'd said not to. He opened the door to find Vicky in shorts and a tank top, rushing into her galley kitchen. From all appearances, she seemed to be trying to catch a massive spray of water with a bath towel. She was soaked to the bone, and the towel—like the ones already on the floor—wasn't doing a damn bit of good.

"Move."

Vicky spun toward his voice, shock on her features, but dived out of the way, giving him access to the sink. The spray drenched him before he'd even knelt down in the narrow space, but at least this part he could fix without a problem. He groped blindly under the sink, feeling for the shutoff valves and twisting them off.

"What are you doing here?"

That so didn't sound like a thank-you. Dante pushed to his feet, no longer caring about the water that was dripping from his clothes. "I said I was coming to help."

"And I told you not to."

"So you would have preferred I hadn't stopped by and let you flood your apartment and the one downstairs?"

"No." She was holding the soaked towel to herself as if it was a shield. Her eyes shifted toward the sink, where a puddle of water sat in the cabinet.

He'd seen the water, the surface tension held it in a bubble right at the lip of the wood. For the moment it was stable, but one more drop, one wrong move, and it would burst and spill onto the floor. "Then what's the problem?"

Drip.

Splash.

"I don't want a hero, Dante. I didn't ask for one, and I don't need one."

Everyone needed a hero sometimes, even him, but he wasn't going to argue with her. "How about a handyman, then? Could you use one of those?"

Vicky bit her lip and gave a resigned nod.

"Good." Dante smiled and held out his hand. "Where are your tools?"

• • •

She'd debated telling him the biggest tool was the one standing right in front of him. After all, what kind of jerk did she have to be to almost refuse the help of a guy who'd driven over from Brentwood just because of her sink? Instead, she simply acquiesced and gave him access to the few tools she had on hand. Brandon had kept most of them, but until now, she'd been sure she had enough — knew enough — to get by.

So she had gone to work on the dripping pipe.

And it turned into a geyser. She'd had no clue. None. The only answer had been towels, and she was pretty much out of those now that she'd used the last one to dry off.

It would have been bad enough if the super had shown to repair the leak, but it had to be Dante racing in to her rescue. One more guy determined to fix things. To make everything right. To take care of her.

To look ridiculously smoking hot as he scooted a few inches under her kitchen sink. He'd taken off his shirt while she was gone, and for the first time since running into him again, she had a perfect view of the body she'd lusted after. With him still twisting a wrench on one of the pipes, he wasn't even going to notice her staring. Or drooling.

The muscles of his arms bulged as he worked the tool. She'd asked once if he'd ever measured them, and he'd only laughed. The one thing she knew for sure was his arm was bigger around than most guys' necks were. And both arms were covered with ink. Most of his tattoos she'd seen before, but she liked the way he'd worked the new one on his chest into his shoulder design.

He had told her the multihued fire reaching up from his elbow was the first piece he'd gotten — shortly after he started wrestling as the Inferno. The flames licked the design above where it looked as if his shoulder had ragged gashes torn through the skin, revealing gears and mechanics running underneath. Those were his older ink.

Since then, he'd let the mechanized theme carry over his chest. Rather than slashes through skin, this was displayed as an open wound—a clockwork heart beating for all to see. The heart bore a jagged line through it, as if the craftsman who'd made Dante had pieced him together from mismatched bits. Man and machine forced into one body.

Vicky frowned. There was another new one below that, right at the edge of the mechanics. It looked like a word, but Dante had twisted away, and she couldn't quite make it out. She needed to know what it said. There was absolutely no logic to it, but the desire had her feet moving before her brain kicked into gear.

"See something you like?"

Vicky jerked her gaze up to Dante's face. He'd scooted out from under the sink while she'd been looking, and there was no hiding her appreciation now—she could feel her nipples straining against her bra and poking happily against the fabric of her wet tank top. "I…was just wondering if you think it's fixed now."

Something strange flickered in his eyes as he smiled at her, but all he said was, "Only one way to be sure."

He twisted the knobs under the sink, and the sound of water moving again made her wince, but there was no more spray. She knelt down on the towels and peeked—dry as dry could be. He'd even mopped up the water that had been in there earlier. "Thank you."

Grunting, Dante pushed to his feet and laid the wrench on the counter. "Not a problem. I can be a rather helpful guy to have around if given the chance."

"I'm starting to see that." As she stood, he was drying his hands on the small kitchen towel, the motion moving his biceps, triceps, and lats in ways that made her want to rub her legs together until she could shove him out the door and have a little one-on-one time with BOB. She strode quickly into the living room, desperate for space. It didn't do any good—her imagination followed her.

And Dante was only a step behind. "Any chance there's an unsoaked towel I can use before I head home to change?"

Vicky tried to shake off her thoughts, but moving on from his muscles only brought her to his soul-stealing eyes. Her mouth went dry with how close he stood, and how close to naked he was. It would take less than a minute to have him undressed and in her bed.

But she wasn't supposed to want that. *Bad news, Vicky. Bad news.*

"Vicky?"

The instant his full lips moved, sounding out her name, she stopped caring about bad news, or any news at all. She stopped caring about BOB or the wet towels on the floor or the fact that her super could walk in at any minute.

After five years of waiting, of wondering—she just wanted his mouth on hers.

She reached out, her fingers tangling in his hair, and crushed her lips against his. It wasn't like the kiss outside Mortensen's house. This wasn't fraught with anything but need, and damn, did she need it. He only hesitated for a second before kissing her back with as much hunger as she felt. The next thing she knew, she was against the wall as his lips carved a path down her neck.

Yes. Yes. And holy hell, yes.

The single word was on repeat in her skull. She wanted this. Needed it.

Her fingernails scraped against his chest, clawing over his mechanical heart on the way to something she already knew was all flesh. She fought with the button on his wet jeans, yanking until she was sure they'd have to cut his pants off. Then his hands were there, too, opening the button and zipper as if they'd just been sealed, waiting for his okay.

She slid her hand under the fabric, shoving it down as she reached for him. He was so hard just touching him made her moan, and as if he'd forgotten about her mouth until the sound, suddenly his lips were on hers again.

There was nothing but the sensation of Dante. His lips, his tongue, his teeth, his cock…

Until the door opened. "Hello? Anyone here? I came to take a look at that plumbing issue."

And like that, the spell was shattered.

What the hell was she doing? Dante was off-limits. Even if he wasn't her brother's best friend. Even if he wasn't *bad news*. Even if he hadn't blackmailed her to go out with him after she'd crawled into bed with him by accident.

He was a client.

He could destroy her.

Vicky yanked her hand out of his pants and ducked under his arm, headed for the door. "My friend came over and took care of it. But if it starts leaking again, is there a plumber I should be calling directly?"

The few minutes talking to the superintendent cooled her blood and got her brain under control. When she turned around, however, she was still faced with a shirtless and sexy as hell Dante.

She bit her lip for a full ten-second count before she said, "You should probably go."

"Vicks…" He stepped toward her with his hand outstretched like he was going to brush it along her cheek or her arm or do something else to soothe away the stress she'd heard in her own voice.

"No. This was a mistake. I'm sorry. We need to work together and we can't… I don't want… This can't happen."

His hand dropped to his side, and he let out a sigh so deep it felt painful. "Why? Just tell me that."

Because I'll let you save me? Because I haven't found my way yet, and you'll just make me get lost again? Because I don't know up from down when I'm with you?

"Because you're a client, Dante, and besides that, I don't know you anymore. I'm not sure I ever really did." And that thought was the one she knew would keep her up tonight. "Please, just go. We'll pretend this never happened and start on the party tomorrow."

Jaw tight, Dante brushed past her and yanked open the door. He stood there for a minute, staring at her before he said, "You know, Vicks, I might be an actor by trade, but I'm not sure I can pull off pretending that never happened. I don't think you can, either."

Then he was gone. She sagged against the wall and raked her hands through her damp hair, certain that no matter how right he might be, she had to try.

Chapter Seven

Dante had left Vicky alone the rest of the day, only texting late that night to ask when and where she wanted to meet for party planning. He'd planned to nudge her about their dating agreement, just to see where things really stood between them, but she saved him the trouble by mentioning it herself.

I HAVEN'T FORGOTTEN WHAT I AGREED TO REGARDING DATING YOU, BUT PUBLIC ONLY FROM NOW ON. THERE WILL BE NO MORE SURPRISING ME AT MY APARTMENT.

He wasn't about to argue, considering she'd given him more than he expected after what had gone down at her place. Still, he had to scramble for somewhere to go, since he'd thought she'd tell him to stick his threats so far up his ass he'd be spitting them out. The one thing he had going for him was she'd made it pretty clear she wanted to get to know him. Lunch at the diner had been part of his past, but they needed more of *that* kind of time together before there could ever be anything deeper.

He'd been planning a sunset walk on the beach to talk, but then he'd gotten a call that put beach-going on the back burner. Not wanting to lose the extra time with Vicky, though, he'd sent a text asking her to wear comfortable clothes and sneakers to their meeting.

They'd stowed her binder and laptop in his trunk and had been driving on the 405 for a while when she said, "So, when do I get to find out where we're headed?"

Debate over the wisdom of what to say lasted only a few seconds. "We're going to see my little brother."

Her brows wrinkled in consternation, and she twisted in her seat to look at him. "You have a brother?"

"Yes. Well, no." He swept a hand through his hair and let the strands flop over his forehead again. "Big Brothers Big Sisters brother. His name's Juan, and he's almost eighteen and not so little anymore." At long last he pulled into the exit lane for Venice Boulevard.

Still seeming confused, Vicky said, "And you want to ask him to the party? We're not at that point yet."

"I wish." The breath he blew out was one of remorse. Things had been going really well for Juan lately, so Dante hadn't come around as much. He should have known better. "His mother called. Juan skipped school today. She's worried."

"Oh." The single syllable said more than if she'd babbled the rest of the drive. It contained half a dozen questions, along with what were likely a few moments of judgment.

"I debated asking you for a rain check on today, but

we already missed party planning yesterday and you need your paycheck. Besides, you said you wanted to get to know me." He shrugged as he pulled to a stop, the seat belt cutting across his shoulder in a way that hurt. Rubbing at the old injury, he gave Vicky a wan smile. "This is part of me."

"What do you mean?" she asked as he turned north toward Venice—the hitch in her voice said she knew the area's reputation. This wasn't a walk on the beach, not by a long shot.

"I didn't grow up here, but home was like this in a lot of ways. Houses might have been a little bigger, but they were more beat-up. And the gangs were just as active. Drugs, prostitution, guns—I grew up with all of it."

"With it? Or *with* it?"

The implication was clear—was she going to regret wanting to know? "A guy down the street saw a bunch of gangbangers talking to me one day when I was about twelve. Came out and chased them off with a fucking rake." He laughed, seeing it again in his head. It had been his cross-roads, that moment, and he'd never been more sure he'd made the right choice about anything in his life. "Never thought those guys would have been scared away by something like a rake, but Mr. Corbitt had more than a touch of crazy in his eyes. I remember growing up, people had said he'd been in Vietnam and came home with multiple pieces of metal buried under his skin. The stories said he refused to let the doctors take them out. That if he'd survived being shot, he could survive keeping the souvenirs."

"Sounds like an interesting guy. Was any of it true?"

Dante drove slowly, looking for a familiar face…or someone jogging in a vain effort to outrun their demons.

"Everything except that he didn't have the slugs taken out. He did keep them, though—in a jar on his desk. He said they reminded him to be thankful he was alive." There. Juan. Right out in the open with his damn basketball. Dante pulled the car toward a free parking spot. It was tight, but he could make it. "Mr. Corbitt took me aside and told me a real man didn't need a gang. A real man made something of himself. He taught me how to fight—boxing, karate…wrestling. In a way, he became my gang. I didn't need those assholes. I had the scariest guy around watching my back. He's the reason I am who I am and not…something else."

She was unbuckling her seat belt the instant he threw the car into park. "Do you ever talk about him in interviews? I've never heard this story before."

"No," Dante said, his hands choking the wheel as he thought about what had happened to Mr. Corbitt. Like Juan, Dante had his own demons, and he held them as close as he could so he never forgot that it was his job to do the right thing—rather than the easy thing. "Some of my past isn't for public consumption."

"Thank you for telling me." She laid a hand on his arm and smiled.

She couldn't know how badly talking about it at all hurt, and he didn't want her to. Getting to know him really meant she wanted to see all the good stuff. The *now* stuff. The past was ugly and would only get in the way. He'd give her enough to understand, but deep down, he was sure she'd never want more than that. More was just…messy. "You wanted to know. But he's the reason I mentor Juan. I wanted to be that for someone else."

"Hence this side trip."

Nodding, he jerked open his door and climbed out of the car. By the time he rounded to Vicky's side, he'd chased away the ghost of Lee Corbitt and could deal with Juan. Or he could try to. At least the kid was alone. That was something.

He took Vicky's hand in his and clicked the alarm on the car. Not that it would stop anyone really determined, but at least he'd get a heads-up if and when it got jacked. The steady *thump-thump-thump* of the basketball was barely interrupted by the occasional *swish*. With all the dribbling, Juan wasn't out here for a pickup game or even to practice. He was thinking—hard.

Dante didn't call out; he didn't want to startle the kid. Damn, Juan was looking skinny. And scruffy. He needed a good meal and a fucking haircut. Rounding to the other side of the basketball court, he approached Juan head-on. "School give you the day off?"

The ball paused, the sudden quiet jarring. "Fuck. Mom called you, didn't she? I told her I had shit going on."

"What kind of shit?" Dante tried to keep his voice even, but he heard the note of accusation sift in anyway.

"Aw, man. Not that." At an arched brow, Juan thrust the ball toward Dante, catching him in the chest. "A scout came to school."

"A scout?" Dante dribbled awkwardly.

"Doesn't matter." Huffing out a breath, Juan held his hands toward the ball.

Dante bounced it off the blacktop, but before it continued on its way to Juan, Vicky caught it. The way Juan's gaze shot toward her was borderline accusatory, like she shouldn't be there. And maybe she shouldn't have been.

Then she spun the ball on a fingertip and gave a crooked

smile. "How about instead of an interrogation, you and I play for answers?"

"Play?" The aggression disappeared, replaced with an amused light.

"Horse. If I make a shot, you have to fill him in"—she cocked her head toward Dante—"with a piece of the puzzle. If you get a shot, you can ask him anything."

Oh, that could end badly.

"What about you? Can I ask you?"

Before Dante could advise her that maybe this wasn't the best idea, she said, "Sure."

Vicky dribbled up to the faded free-throw line, and the ball soared into the net. Juan came toward her with the ball, but she wouldn't budge. "You owe an answer first."

"I didn't miss yet."

"That wasn't the deal. The horse part only determines when we're done. Faster someone loses, the faster the game's over. So what do you want more? Your pride or your privacy?" She crossed her arms over her chest and nodded toward Dante.

Grumbling something in Spanish, Juan spat, "A basketball scout came to school, said he'd heard things about me." He waved a hand toward the free-throw line. Vicky moved out of the way, and he made the shot as easily as she had. The ball hit the post and bounced back toward him. He thrust it at Vicky. "First question, who the hell is she?"

"Parole officer?" At Juan's glare, Dante held his hands up. "It was a joke. She's Evan's sister and a friend."

"I'm also his party planner, but he likes to forget I have a job." Vicky stepped outside the three-point line and made another shot.

"Lady, you're going to have to try harder at some point or this is going to get really boring."

"Out of practice, hotshot. Give a girl a minute." She grabbed the ball, leaving him time to talk.

Slowly, over the course of many shots both made and missed, Vicky got Juan to admit he'd been recruited by a college. One on the East Coast. "Not sure how I feel about leaving Mom here on her own."

Dante shook his head. He knew Juan's mother and how hard she worked to keep her kids in school and out of trouble. A college education for him would be her dream come true. "Talk to her instead of worrying her. She thinks you're looking to join a gang."

"Isn't that what college is? A huge gang of smart people?"

Dante shook his head. "If that's what you really believe, maybe you don't deserve that scholarship. Maybe you want to stay here your whole life. Be the guy who hustles tourists for money on the beach? Or is it worse than that?"

"Fuck you, man." Juan ripped the ball from Vicky's grasp, rushed the net, and slammed it through. "Last question." He pointed at her. "Why the fuck are you here with him?"

For the first time since they'd arrived, Dante turned his attention to her. Juan would either take what he said to heart or not, but she'd not only seen this side of his life, she'd joined right in. And she'd been pretty amazing. Mr. Corbitt would have been as impressed as Dante was, maybe more. Now, her cheeks were slightly flushed from the game, and her hair was sticking to her neck. She gave a gentle shake of her head. "I don't really know, but I think I might be starting to figure it out."

. . .

"So now what? This isn't exactly the way back to the city." In Dante's car again after watching Juan head toward home, Vicky rolled down the window, letting the breeze blow her hair back and dry the thin stream of sweat on her face.

"I'd planned on taking you to the beach." He pointed out the windshield as if she could see the ocean from here.

She chuckled. "Might have told me to bring a suit."

"Well, the original plan was to work on the party and then do a sunset picnic on the beach." He waved toward the empty backseat. "If you notice, I forgot the picnic basket."

"But we're still going to the beach?"

"Unless you have a better plan." He turned onto Neilson Way and started driving north, putting Venice in the rearview.

Sunset on the beach sounded far too romantic for bad-news-Dante-who-blackmailed-her-to-date-him-and-she-almost-fucked-in-her-living-room-last-night. But it sounded kind of amazing with the guy she'd been seeing snapshots of in between.

The dichotomy confused the hell out of her. The Dante she'd been getting to know didn't seem the type who would destroy a woman for rejecting him. So why the hell had he threatened to do it to her? And what had yesterday been? Sure, she'd been the aggressor, but he hadn't even tried to put on the brakes. *Exactly* like when she'd crawled in his bed by mistake.

Obviously, there was the possibility that Dante-the-wonderful was an act. Actors lied for a living. She knew the reality well from being Evan's sister, but she'd also seen it since she'd started working for Elegant Entertainment. Most didn't go so far as to spend the kind of money he was dropping on this party to solidify the lie, though.

Under other circumstances, the back-and-forth would have given her a headache, but she was riding along with the ocean breeze raking fingers of wind through her hair while sitting next to one of the sexiest guys in the world. Even if acting like he really cared was all a lie, it was one she was stuck inside for a while.

And what if—after yesterday, she was afraid to even acknowledge the possibility—but what if the threat had been the lie? She still couldn't figure out why he'd do that, but if it was the lie and this was the truth…

She wasn't supposed to get involved either way, but part of her wanted to know more, to know *him* more. And even friendship meant getting involved. She blew out a slow breath and tried to focus on anything other than the man sitting next to her. Friendship *didn't* involve romantic picnics on the beach, so that was out no matter what.

Then she caught sight of the Santa Monica Pier and remembered talking to Stasia about dating Evan. They'd started their whirlwind romance at an amusement park. Granted, Stasia hadn't given details about how things had gone after that, but now they were married and ridiculously happy.

Vicky wasn't naive enough to believe the roller coasters had made them fall in love, but hanging at an amusement park was definitely more friend territory than the option he'd presented.

She laid a hand on Dante's arm to get his attention, then tipped her head toward the view ahead. "I haven't been to

Pacific Park since we first moved out here with Evan. What do you say? Want to take me on an amusement park date?" She almost flinched as she said "date," but that had been their two-week agreement anyway. She could pretend she was just playing along rather than slipping up because it felt right. Too right.

"Are you asking *me* out?"

"Nope. I'm asking you to win me a giant stuffed animal and get me sticky with cotton candy. Duh."

His lips twisted into a smirk that he couldn't seem to hold back from breaking into a full-on grin. "When you put it that way, how could I resist?"

A few minutes later, they were parked and walking hand in hand toward the pier. Dante had thrown on a baseball cap to go with his sunglasses. It would have looked ridiculous if it weren't still so bright. No one would give the combo a second thought on a day like today. She pulled an elastic out and swept her hair into a messy bun. Dante raised a brow. She planted her hands on her hips and frowned. "What?"

"Nothing. It's just not a look I would have ever expected to like."

"But you do?"

"I do."

Laughing, she rolled her eyes. "Weirdo."

He held out his hand and waited as she stared, finally saying, "I'm less likely to be noticed by people if they see us as a couple."

"And that means we won't get mobbed by your fans." She stared a second longer, then wrapped her fingers in his, trying desperately to ignore the electricity that raced up her arm. It was a stupid, innocent touch, one she could pretend meant nothing. "Lead on, boyfriend."

"Careful, a guy could get used to that."

So could she. "Fine. Lead on, jerkface."

He frowned at her for a second and then burst out laughing as he tugged her toward the pier. "Well, I definitely won't get the wrong idea now."

Chapter Eight

Before they made it to the park entrance, the sound of at least a dozen dogs barking met them, and Vicky yanked him to a stop. He looked around, confused. "What's wrong?"

Her eyes lit up like a kid's on Christmas morning, and she pointed to a sign off to the left—ADOPTION EVENT. "Can we? Please?"

Between location shoots and his busy schedule when he was home, the last thing Dante needed in his life was a dog. But maybe Vicky wanted one. "As long as you don't try to push me into saving them all. I'm not a canine warrior."

She wrinkled her nose at him. "Some superhero you turned out to be." Dropping his hand, she practically skipped up to the temporary fencing.

It didn't take long before she was nose to nose with a spotted mutt that looked like some weird combination of dalmatian and pit bull. Dante strode over, and the animal's tail stopped moving as it eyed him, immediately alert.

"Friendly thing, huh?"

"She was until you got here." Vicky reached through the fence and stroked the dog's head. "It's okay, girl. I know he looks big and tough, but he's really an old softie. You should have him tell you about Diner Fries and his first job."

Dante laughed but watched as the dog returned its full attention to Vicky. A few minutes later, a shelter rep came over and asked, "Are you interested in Jinx?"

Vicky's joy melted away. "I wish I could be, but my apartment complex doesn't allow animals. And my ex was allergic, so as always, I have to get my doggy love through the fence."

"Oh, I'm sorry to hear that." The rep walked away, looking almost as sad as Vicky had.

While she and the dog bonded, Dante went after the rep. "Hey, I couldn't help but notice your reaction back there."

The rep gave a sad smile. "I know Jinx will make someone a wonderful pet. Problem is…she's a handful and not an easy fit." The kid glanced toward the pen and then jerked his head forward again. "Her time's up tomorrow. I begged to get her included in today's event as one last chance, you know?"

He didn't know, not where animals were concerned, but he understood last chances. That's what acting had been for him after… After. If Vicky knew the dog was going to be euthanized tomorrow, she'd never forgive him for leaving it behind. Cursing himself, he pulled out a card and scribbled his number on the back. "This is going to sound stupid, but I want you to keep me updated on her. If someone adopts her, I want to know. If she's still here at the end of the day, I want to know that, too."

The kid nodded, frowning as he took in the front of the

card. "Holy shit. You're the Inferno?"

Not anymore. "Yeah. Just keep it quiet that I'm here, okay? Text me about Jinx."

"Sure thing, but I'm totally spilling tomorrow that I met you."

"Tomorrow's fine. I'd just prefer to stay incognito today." And he'd prefer to not have Vicky's heart break over something he could save. He wasn't sure how, or where, but one way or another, that dog was finding a home.

• • •

They spent an hour with the dogs, but Vicky knew her reality wouldn't allow her to have a pet. She only hoped someone saw how friendly Jinx was and gave the adorable mutt a chance. Walking away was made marginally easier by the fact that a little boy took her place at the fence, seeming to take a shine to the dog right off.

Still, she laced her fingers in Dante's in some strange effort to hold off sadness. Someday things would be stable, and she'd have a place where she could have a dog. Maybe a cat, too. For now, regardless of everything else, the guy by her side was trying to help her on that path. It would have to be enough.

Immediately upon entering the park, Dante headed to the games. "Is this the part where you make me play every game so you can give me grief over the ones I suck at?"

He must have heard the stories about Evan and Stasia, too. Either that or he'd noticed how bummed she was about Jinx and was trying to distract her. She could play along. "Nope. I just figure the size of the prize will show how much you want me to go out with you again."

"And a bunch of smaller ones won't cut it?" The way he tipped his head toward hers said her answer mattered a lot more to him than it should. "Is this like the size of the diamond in an engagement ring or something?"

And…that was not a conversation they should've been having, not even in the vaguest sense. "Well, engagement is *not* an option, and if it were, I don't want a diamond anyway. So, yeah. In this, I demand the most humongous prize available."

"Fine. But when I get you that prize, you have to agree to attend an event with me tomorrow for my charity." He tugged her past most of the games, ignoring Tub Toss, Water Race, and Mini-hoops. Clearly, he had a specific destination in mind.

"Okay, but where are we going in such a hurry?"

"You said the biggest prize available. Those are here." He stopped and waved toward the booth to his right: Riptide Ring Toss.

He was right—the jumbo prizes in the booth were the largest she had seen, and there was even an adorable giant penguin. "Ring toss, though? Does anyone ever win this game?"

As soon as she said the words, she caught herself. This was her way out of further dates. Things with Dante could become all business if he failed here. So, why did the idea of him losing stress her out suddenly? They could still be friends without the dates and the stupid sexual tension. If it was all business, she could force herself to stop thinking about where dating usually led, where they'd almost gone twice already.

Dante threw a hand over his heart as if she'd wounded him. "You doubt me?"

"I doubt the game."

Laughing, he handed a ten to the barker running the booth. "Keep a count. I'm playing until I win the lady a prize—however many buckets it takes." He took his bucket of rings and leaned close to Vicky, his breath feathering her hair as he whispered, "All the games have tricks to make them more winnable, but do you want to know the real trick—the thing that makes the difference between walking away with a big stuffed animal and not just lighter in the pocket?"

"What is it?" she said on a breath, trying to figure out why her arms were breaking out in gooseflesh and why she wanted to lean into him.

"The same thing that gets you anything in life…perseverance." He tossed the first ring, flicking his wrist as he let go. It spun but bounced off a bottle and slid between them. "Well, that and a bit of luck."

With every toss, Vicky wanted to take back the challenge. She didn't need a damn stuffed animal. Dante was on the last ring from his bucket, and her heart was hammering. *Stupid charity event. I probably don't even want to go. The party planning's the important thing, right?*

Dante tipped his head toward her and said with a grin, "I'd ask for a kiss for luck, but I have this sinking feeling you won't—"

There was no thought involved on Vicky's end. She grabbed him by the collar of his shirt, yanked him toward her, and pressed her lips against his. It didn't begin as anything romantic. It was just some strange form of desperation that sprang from her mouth, yet still different from the kiss in her apartment.

Then a piece of the wall she had built around herself in the aftermath of her divorce shattered, and she yielded against him, pressing her body to the length of his and twining her arms around his neck. She'd heard of magical kisses, but she'd never experienced anything like one until now, until the moment his tongue teased at the seam of her lips, and not a single sliver of her being could resist opening to him.

He claimed her mouth, not through any force or demand, but by gradually accepting every inch she offered. There was no struggle, no fear, no doubt. There was only the momentary fusion of two souls.

And then it was over.

Eyes dark with a desire she was sure matched her own, Dante whispered, "How could I ever ask for more than that?" Then, with a flick of his wrist, he let the last ring fly.

Vicky's heart almost stopped as she watched it sail over the bottles, spinning so fast it was little more than a red blur. It bounced off one bottle, killing the spin...and fell onto another, swirling over the mouth of the thing before it settled around it.

"Like I said, Vicks, perseverance and luck. Thanks for the latter." He dropped a gentle peck on her nose, then waved at the carny. "I do believe the lady gets a prize."

The next thing she knew, she had a giant stuffed penguin under one arm and her other around Dante's waist as he fed her cotton candy. For a moment, she felt like a teenager again. Like there'd been no wasted marriage, no divorce, no need to put her life back together because she was just starting it now, and for this snapshot of time—it was perfect.

If she examined it too long, the idea terrified her, but

just this once, she wanted to forget all the other things in her life and just…live.

"You know what would make this impromptu date even better?" she asked, feeling far braver than she had any reason to.

"What?" Dante shoved a huge bite of cotton candy in her mouth as if daring her to try to talk around it.

She let it melt, then swatted him on his ridiculously hard pecs. "Just because of doing that, now you *have to* take me on the Ferris wheel before we leave."

Dante jerked to a stop. "The Ferris wheel?"

She nodded. "You can see forever from the top. I've always thought it would be incredibly romantic to take a ride on it and get stuck up there for hours." The fact that she'd been avoiding romance with him until this moment seemed blissfully unimportant.

"Sure, until one of you needs to go to the bathroom."

She laughed, the sound freer than she could remember it being in a long time. "Thanks for spoiling the fantasy moment with a big stinking pile of reality. Come on. One ride? Then we can figure out a way to half-ass that picnic on the beach."

After ditching the now empty bag of cotton candy, Dante scrubbed at his face and dragged a hand through his hair. "One ride and we're done?"

"Yeah."

"Okay, but if we get stuck at the top for hours, I'm holding you personally responsible."

Well, if they got stuck at the top for hours, odds were she'd end up giving in to temptation and kissing him again. Only this time she wasn't sure she'd want to stop. And she was more than willing to take full responsibility for that.

• • •

Right before they boarded, Dante's phone buzzed. The family who had visited with Jinx after Vicky was taking her home. That was the high point of the moment. He was staring down the low as it swung to a stop in front of them. Bright yellow and about as cheerful as could be, the Ferris wheel car made him want to run back to the dogs—or his own car.

He plastered on as brave a face as he could muster and climbed aboard anyway. The door hadn't even shut to lock them in yet, and Dante could feel himself turning green. *Way to impress her, dumbass—let her see you at your absolute worst when things have finally taken a really fantastic turn.*

As the Ferris wheel car swung into motion, he tried to focus on the kiss. That amazing press of lips on lips, the dance of tongues—the meaning behind it. When he'd mentioned a kiss for luck, getting one was the last thing he'd expected. And his luck had been crap.

While ring toss was completely rigged against the player, it had been one of those stupid things he'd taken it on himself to learn how to beat. He almost always won within fifteen tosses. He'd paid for a full fucking bucket. On the last ring, he'd been sure fate was telling him this was all over, that if he walked away from Vicky now, she'd be safe from Reed. Since that had been his goal in the beginning, he would have taken his lumps and let her go, secure in the knowledge that she wouldn't be one of that asshole's victims.

Then he'd have found some way to nurse his libido back to life.

But she'd kissed him. More than kissed him, really. It was as if she was as afraid of him losing the game as he was. It had given him more than luck in the end. It had given him hope.

And then she'd thrown the damned Ferris wheel on top of that magical moment.

The car tilted back and forth as the wheel moved to pick up the next load of passengers, and Dante closed his eyes. *It's only a few minutes. You can survive a few minutes without making yourself look like a total ass.*

"Are you okay?"

Or not. Dante gritted his teeth as he forced a smile. "Sure. Never better. Why do you ask?"

She tipped her head toward the plastic bench. "Because your knuckles are turning white from gripping the edge of the seat so hard."

He tried to make himself let go, but he couldn't. Clearly, he would have to admit the truth or look like an even bigger idiot for trying to hide something so obvious. "Fine. I'm afraid of heights—particularly the ones that won't kill you but will maim you for life."

"Then why did you agree to do this?"

"Because you wanted to do it." He shrugged like it should have been as obvious as his fear, but the move was hampered by the way he was attached to the ride.

"That either makes you the biggest dork in the world or the biggest sweetheart."

She stood, and Dante blanched, mentally seeing her topple over the edge of the car and plummet to the ground. "Sit down! Do you want to get yourself killed?"

Lips twisted into a smirk, Vicky perched on the edge

of the seat and shuffled her way toward him. "There? Happier?" She peeled the fingers of one of his hands from the plastic, then snuggled close so he was forced to choose between holding onto the Ferris wheel car and holding her.

There was no choice. His hand snaked over her back to find her waist and squeeze her even tighter to his side. "Mildly happier."

She snorted a laugh and buried her face against his chest. "What would a girl have to do to make you *much* happier?"

"Make me forget I'm dangling in a metal box hundreds of feet from the ground?"

She snuggled in closer. "Okay, let's try talking. Look at me and tell me all about this charity thing we're going to."

The instant the wheel jerked into motion again, he turned her way. God, she was beautiful. Against the backdrop of the distant setting sun, her hair was aglow in a golden corona of light. His own personal angel. "You're going with me then?"

"After making you get on this thing? I don't really feel like I have much of a choice." She rolled her eyes like he should have known her response. "So where are we off to? One of those things where we work at the local McDonald's? Car wash?"

"Well, now I'm wishing it was a car wash just for the chance to get you in a bikini."

"Very funny."

It might have been, but it was also enticing. He didn't deserve the pieces of her he was getting, but that didn't stop him from wanting more. And didn't stop his dick from responding to thoughts of her in only a couple scraps of fabric. Time to focus on reality before he made a fool of himself again. "Never fault a man for being honest when he answers a question. No car wash…this time. We're going to the opera instead."

"Opera?"

He nodded. "Several student musicians we kept off the street will be performing with the pit orchestra as guests. It started as a small thing, but then word got around and we sold out the theater. It's turned out to be a really big deal." Lee would have loved it. The guest performances were exactly the kind of thing he'd have tried to arrange for Dante had his skill set been music rather than violence. But Lee knew him on sight. Kindred spirits and all that. He'd left the damn bullet fragments to Dante in his will.

"Opera." She shook her head, tearing him from the dark memory and back to her light. "I don't have anything to wear to the damned opera." Vicky started worrying at the nail of her index finger. "Maybe Stasia left something at Evan's place here that'll fit."

"Or I can get something for you." The idea of buying something for her—providing for her—gave him a much bigger thrill than he wanted to admit.

"No."

"Vicky…"

"I said no. That's a silly waste of money, especially since Stasia and I are pretty much the same size."

And then the Ferris wheel started moving in earnest, and the time for arguing passed. His fingers clenched at her skin, and Vicky made sure he had no way to disagree with her—by covering his lips with hers.

By the time the ride stopped, he'd almost forgotten why buying her a gown was such a big deal.

Almost.

Chapter Nine

One of the biggest reasons Dante wanted Vicky at the opera was because it had nothing to do with the birthday party, the movie, or even Reed. More specifically, he really wanted her to have a chance to see him away from Hollywood and closer to something near and dear to his heart.

I don't have anything to wear to the damned opera.

At least the issue hadn't changed her answer to a no. He'd still been unsteady after the Ferris wheel—even with all her distractions. In the end, he'd asked if she'd take a rain check for the picnic on the beach. Since she'd needed to get in touch with Stasia about a dress anyway, she'd agreed.

By the time Dante made it home, he regretted the decision.

A smart man would have said, let's just find a nice, quiet restaurant. A smart man would have taken the whole making-out-on-the-Ferris-wheel bit and run with it all the way home.

He was feeling pretty fucking stupid as his phone buzzed

with an incoming text.

PROBLEM. STASIA IS SUCH A CONSCIENTIOUS HOLLYWOOD
WIFE THAT SHE ALREADY DONATED ALL HER DRESSES TO CHARITY.
WHAT ARE THE REQUIREMENTS FOR SOMETHING LIKE THIS? I
STILL HAVE SOME TIME TO GO OUT SHOPPING. ALSO, CAN WE AT
LEAST DO SOME EMAILING BACK AND FORTH ABOUT THE PARTY SO
I HAVE A FEW BILLABLE HOURS FOR TODAY?

Just knowing she was willing to go out of her way—and
spend money she really didn't have—to attend the event
with him made Dante realize that pushing her toward more
intimacy would have cheapened what they already had. The
kissing was enough until she made it clear she was ready for
more. He just hoped that happened soon. He texted back:

SEND ME YOUR ADDRESS AND YOUR DRESS SIZE. MEASURE-
MENTS IF YOU CAN. THEN I'LL EMAIL BACK ABOUT THE PARTY.

She'd balked a little but had agreed in the end. And,
after laying out some party basics for a couple hours, he'd
gone to sleep with a smile on his face. Now, in the light of
day, he was nervous again. He'd called in a favor to a friend
who worked as a personal shopper. She'd promised to take
care of everything for Vicky.

But there'd been no contact since then. He shouldn't
be nervous, but it felt like picking up his date for prom or
something.

With the limo at the curb, waiting to take them to the airport, and all her neighbors poking noses out doors or shifting open blinds, Dante strode to Vicky's door and knocked.

She stepped out, a vision in bronze satin. The top of the dress, with ruching on the sides, was held up by a single shoulder strap, and the plain skirt was slit nearly to her hip. Frowning, she waved toward the people watching them. "Seriously? You couldn't have called up from the car? Or better yet, let me take a cab to the airport? I was going to get enough looks walking out in a designer gown. It's kind of hard to not deal with prying questions when your date picks you up in a limo. It's even harder when your date makes it obvious to everyone that he's famous."

"If you really want to make it look like it's not a big deal, I can take care of that." He grinned at her, then turned toward the courtyard and said as loudly as possible, "Hi, everyone, I'm Dante Palladino, and I wanted to thank you for checking us out. Doesn't Vicky look gorgeous? My friend here won a raffle to be my date tonight—all the proceeds from the event we're attending go to my charity to keep kids in school and off the streets. Don't worry, I promise to have your neighbor back safe and sound as well. Have a great night."

When he turned back to Vicky, her cheeks were stained crimson. "Yeah. That was a lot more subtle."

"Perfect." He winked, getting far too much enjoyment out of her being flustered than he should have. Hell, he was just glad she hadn't backed out. "Are we ready to go then?"

"Lead on." She hesitated when he offered his arm, but slid her fingers against his bicep—obviously aware her neighbors were still watching. "Nice plug for the charity, by the way. Could you have done the whole minimizing thing without the self-promotion?"

The self— What the hell *had* she read about him in

the past few years to even remotely think he was that kind of guy? "The easiest way for people to find out where the money is going is with my name. The easiest way for us to find out what is most effective with the kids is through people who live in troubled neighborhoods. It's a circle that works, Vicky."

Dante held the limousine door open for her, but she stopped before entering and turned to look at him. "I'm sorry. I just… I'm trying to figure out who the hell you are, and *nothing* is meshing with anything else in my head. The smart part of me says I shouldn't care, but I'm starting to, and it's driving me crazy."

Boxing her in with his arms, Dante leaned close and whispered in her ear, "There's an easy way to find out what you want to know. It's called asking."

. . .

Asking. Yeah. Right. It was like he forgot her brother was an actor, too. They lied for a living. It'd be far too easy for him to say whatever he wanted her to believe. And, unlike growing up with Evan, she hadn't known Dante all her life. She couldn't recognize his tells.

The only thing she knew for sure was that, other than the original blackmail threat, she hadn't seen *anything* bad from him. On the contrary, even when she'd sneaked into his room or shoved her hand in his pants, he'd been a perfect gentleman—which wasn't helping her confusion any at all. Nor was it helping her keep her distance.

She'd come home last night, and after texting about the dress, she'd stewed through two hours of party emails. She'd attempted to distract herself with TV, then a book, then looking at vendors for the party. Anything to settle her mind.

In the end, she'd caved and done an internet search on Dante. The initial hunt hadn't turned up anything she didn't already know: bio, filmography, wrestling history, the charity.

No one's past was that clean.

So she'd searched his name and rumors.

Suddenly there was plenty of reading.

Former wrestling colleagues had called him out for excessive violence in the ring. Some even suggested drug use, though he'd taken every test requested without complaint and passed them all.

A couple costars reportedly bitched about him being an attention whore and provided examples to "prove" it.

Ex-girlfriends.

Tabloid nonsense.

But that was something else she knew because of her brother. A lot of the stories were complete fiction. Unfortunately, some of them usually had a grain of truth. So where was Dante's grain?

She'd worried at the question all night, and then she'd gone and made that *stupid* comment before getting in the limo. He was giving her the princess treatment, and she was acting like some sort of spoiled brat—never getting exactly what she wanted, so she bitched about everything.

But when the limo drove straight up to the plane and Dante took her hand to help her out, she didn't see the guy who blackmailed her. When he kept his hand seated on the small of her back as they boarded the ramp, there wasn't even a glimpse of the violence she'd read about. When he gave her a brief tour of the plane he called "an indulgence he couldn't resist," there were no ex-girlfriends. There was just the two of them, couched in leather seats, alternately staring at each other and looking out the windows at the clouds as they passed by.

He hadn't poked again about how she could ask him anything, which was nice, but she wanted to know. She just didn't know what the hell she was supposed to ask him. And she still hadn't figured out why any of it mattered to her so damn much anyway.

Then his fingers brushed an errant lock of hair from her cheek. She met his gaze, and she understood. It was the same thing she'd known back before she got married, why she'd been so very willing to latch onto Evan's insistence that Dante was bad news.

She was falling for him. Falling for the muscles and the tattoos and the carefree grin. For the guy who moved to L.A. with nothing but an odd skill set and determination. The guy who called his first bosses here his family and had a "little brother" he was trying to nudge toward a better future.

Back before Brandon, she hadn't known most of that stuff about Dante, but he'd charmed her and made her feel smart and beautiful.

Here he was doing it again. Only this time there was no fiancé waiting in the wings and no Evan to tell her to run the other direction. Without all of that, she was hunting for something—anything—to keep her from leaping from a building just to see if Dante would catch her.

The look in his deep brown eyes said he would—without question or worry for his own safety. He'd be there for her.

And the thought was terrifying.

Since Brandon, her main goal had been to get herself

squared away. Sure, she'd dated. She'd even had fun on some of the dates. As Jade knew too well, though, she hadn't had sex—going on two years now—and she certainly hadn't let any guy within a stone's throw of her heart. It wasn't so much that it was still broken as the organ still felt too *breakable*, like with the slightest hint of something off, it would shatter into more pieces than she could possibly reassemble again. Brandon had done that to her—willfully. He'd turned her into a shell of a person, more fragile than she'd ever imagined possible.

Then Dante came along. That night at the party, she'd heard Evan's voice in her head, warning her away from him. But more than that, she'd remembered Dante's magnetic pull on her. She hadn't given in before, but part of her knew she wouldn't be able to resist this time.

For crying out loud, she'd ended up in bed with him that night. Ready to have sex with him, thinking he was another guy. Who the hell did that sort of thing happen to?

It was as if the universe itself was shoving the two of them together. As much as she liked to believe in destiny, she had a hard time thinking that fate wasn't playing a cruel joke on her. After all, he was her brother's best friend and the guy who had almost made her second-guess her impending marriage.

Come to think of it, that last bit might be the very reason she should give him a chance. Had she followed her impulses then, she never would have married Brandon...or let him break her heart.

"Vicks?"

She shook off her musings to find Dante still staring at her, worry in his eyes now. Worry. For her. The fact he could feel that when she'd really been kind of bitchy to him with her whole yes-then-no roller coaster said a lot about his character. Maybe there was some truth to the rumors. Maybe there wasn't. But she needed to stop looking for the bad and start truly embracing the good. There was no question she would let go of her fears eventually—her heart already knew. Her head needed to stop denying it. "Sorry. Lost in my thoughts."

He gave her hand a squeeze that sent sudden, intense need rushing through her body. "Well, if it's anything you want to share, I can be a pretty good sounding board."

"No. I think this is something I have to decide for myself." But she'd already decided. Her reaction to his hand on hers proved it. Now she just needed to figure out how the hell she was supposed to handle the rest of the evening with him when she'd finally given her body free rein to feel everything it had been trying to hold in since seeing him at Saul Mortensen's party.

"Oh. Okay." He let out a breath that probably wasn't meant to sound like a sigh but totally did. "We should be landing in a few minutes. You might want to at least finish your champagne."

She stared at the glass and watched as a bubble separated from the bottom, sliding up through the liquid. It reached the top, and it was as if time stopped, holding its breath for a moment. Then the bubble burst.

Vicky couldn't help but imagine a bubble of desire inside her. It, too, was just waiting for the moment it would escape and she'd get the release she'd been waiting on for such a ridiculously long time.

Waiting…for Dante.

. . .

They made it through the requisite schmoozing of donors large and small and posed for more pictures than Dante wanted to count. This was the part of his job that Lee would have rolled his eyes at. It had taken Dante a long time to realize it wasn't about accolades for doing the right thing so much as advertising for the charity. The pictures garnered them attention, which drew donations, which let them do more good. A positive cycle to break the negative one so many kids found themselves in.

And in this case, it was pictures with Vicky by his side. While Lee might have frowned at the promo, he would have liked her, Dante was sure of it. Looking over at her now, he wondered how on earth anyone *couldn't* like her.

Except the photographer, which made Dante like him less.

When the guy mentioned visible panty lines, Vicky had tried to step away, reminding Dante that no one knew or cared who she was anyway. He'd leaned in close and whispered that he cared. It had been enough to keep her by his side, smiling for photo after photo—after a brief visit to the ladies' room. There'd been no complaints about panty lines after that. The picky photographer would just have to edit out the growing bulge in his pants.

The only exception to her agreeing to be photographed had been promotional shots with the kids who were performing tonight. On that issue, Vicky wouldn't budge. "You're the one who got them here. You're the one their friends will go gaga over. I'm just your date. Get over there and give them the picture they really want."

Something in the way she said it made him cave. It wasn't about her not wanting to be with him—this was her putting the kids first, and that wasn't a motivation he was willing to ignore. Instead, he made a point of introducing her to each and every one of the kids before sending them backstage.

After that, they'd finally made their way to the box Dante had purchased for tonight. He'd planned on inviting some of the other kids—the ones who were on the fence about what they could do with their futures if they applied themselves. Apparently, "opera" was the kiss of death when it came to convincing them of anything. The promise of a ride in a private jet might have enticed a few, but having them hate the opera itself would have been counterproductive.

Until Vicky, he'd imagined sitting in the box all alone. As it was, they stepped through the red velvet curtains into a very secluded seating area.

She glanced around, her hands twisting the clutch purse. "This is cozy."

He arched a brow at her, wondering once more what the hell path they were on as far as she was concerned. She never ran cold, but hot and tepid were still too far apart for his liking. "Want me to invite some people to join us?" He would if it would make her feel better.

"No. I just..." She pressed her lips together, letting them roll free slowly. When she stopped, they were wet and swollen—totally kissable.

"What is it?"

Again, she drew his gaze to her mouth by biting the side of her lower lip. He wanted it in between his own lips so badly, he ached with need—a sensation that was rapidly traveling lower than his mouth. There was no way he'd be able to hide an erection in this damn monkey suit, either.

Finally, she broke the moment by saying, "I never pictured you as a tuxedo guy. Something about the tattoos"—she ran a hand up his arm—"and the hair"—her fingers raked through it, and she smiled as part of it fell across his forehead again. "I don't understand why, exactly, but the combination of all of it… You look really nice." She stepped away, as if she'd done something wrong.

He caught her wrist. "Don't."

She blinked at his fingers. "Don't what?"

Even her voice was tense now. He let go of her arm, then used a single finger to tip her chin back up. "Don't move away from me when everything about you says you want to get closer. And if you don't want that, don't pretend you do. Just be real with me, Vicks. That's all I'll ever ask of you."

Her stance shifted, as if she were rubbing her legs together. "And if I don't know what I want?"

Seemed like he wasn't the only one in need of a little adjustment. He wasn't about to push her, though. He knew Vicky Stone well enough to be sure of one thing: if he pushed, she'd run away. "If that's the case, know that I'll be here when you figure it out."

Chapter Ten

Everything was so much easier when she'd had Dante in her mental bad news lockbox. It wasn't good, but it was easier. They could banter and even flirt so long as there were heavy doses of snark involved. But now that she'd left a door open for him, she couldn't stop seeing him as something more.

She'd watched him all through the first act. He reacted to the music like no one she'd ever seen before. It was as if the notes seeped into his skin until he felt it straight in his soul.

She wanted to be the music…to touch him like that.

Instead, she'd spent the entire time resisting the urge to jump him right there in the private box. By the time the curtain came down, she was throbbing with need and so wet she worried about stains on the dress. Maybe she could sneak to the bathroom and at least put her damn panties back on.

Dante stood and stretched, arching his back. "Are you

enjoying it?"

Still thinking about sex, it took her a minute to register what he meant. "The opera? Yeah. It's lovely."

"Really? Tuberculosis and unrequited love do it for you?"

"I...meant the music." Vicky caught herself twisting her hands in the skirt of her dress, the fabric shifting to reveal a lot more leg than she planned. Another couple inches and it would be more than leg, too. "I'm...going to run to the ladies' room."

"So that's it, huh?" His smile was lopsided this time, not quite cocky but not his full-on grin, either.

"What?"

"What you want." He tipped his head toward her lap. "You're even more on edge than you were before the opera started, but your answer is to go to the bathroom."

Vicky's hand was in motion, ready to straighten out her skirt, when she paused and looked around. "Dante, we're at the opera. Even if I wanted something else, what would you have me do?" *Give you a lap dance while the show goes on below?* "I get that it's a private box, but we're still totally visible here." To prove her point, she swept a hand toward people on the far side of the mezzanine with their cameras out.

Waving to the camera wielders, Dante pulled Vicky to her feet and smiled. "Pretend they can't see us."

"Easier said than done. I found out about Evan and Stasia because of some asshole with a camera. I'd prefer not to make that a family tradition. Mom got over him doing it. I don't think she'd be so easy on me."

"I didn't say anything about getting caught on camera, Vicks. What I want to know is if you had nothing to worry about, what is it you'd want right now?" Dante wrapped an arm around her waist and pulled her close.

She couldn't blame it on tricks of the shadows up here now. The bulge in his pants was a real thing. A really hard thing, and it was pressed against her, making her desire spin out of control. She barely breathed as she said, "I'd ask you to bend me over the rail and take me."

Dante leaned closer, nuzzling her neck until her eyes rolled back in her head. "That's just begging for people to ignore the stage, even when the lights go down again. Other options?"

One of his hands was on the small of her back, holding her tight to him. The other…the other was on her hip, less than an inch from the top of the slit in her skirt. Seconds away from touching her and dousing at least a little of the fire within.

The lights flashed overhead, signaling everyone to return to their seats, but that was the last thing Vicky wanted. If she had to be that close to Dante without anything to give her release, she was sure she'd go crazy. Consequences be damned, she needed him.

Trembling, she laid her hand over his, pushing it toward and then through the slit in her dress. He was *right there*. All he had to do was take what she was offering. "I don't care how you touch me, Dante, but what I really want? I want you. That's all. Nothing else."

• • •

Dante didn't consider saying no for even a second. Instead, the hand on the small of her back moved up to capture her neck and pull her toward him. He slanted his mouth over hers, catching the low groan as he pressed his thumb against her clit. Just then, the theater lights dimmed and the orchestra started up again.

Without a word, he led her from the edge of the box back behind the curtains that hid the less-than-attractive door from sight. There, he pinned her against the velvet-lined wall and trailed kisses over her shoulders and up her neck. "Lift up your dress."

"Here? But the opera…"

He bit down on the sensitive flesh just below her ear-lobe and she moaned, the sound lost in the swelling orchestra music. "We can hear the opera just fine, which means no one will hear you." He eased his hand through the slit and pressed his thumb against her clitoris again, rubbing in slow circles. "You lift up your dress, or the way I'm touching you right now is all you're ever going to get. And we both want more than that."

It was an empty threat, and he was sure she knew it as well as he did, but knowledge didn't seem to matter much when compared to the risk of being wrong. Her hands shook the whole time, but Vicky gathered the satin in her fists, lifting it higher and higher.

He stepped back, drinking her in. The lighting back here was dim, just enough to cast shadows and highlights on her skin, but Dante swore he'd never seen Vicky more beautiful. The heels she wore caused her legs to go tight, muscles flexing in ways that made more blood divert to his dick. And then she moved the dress higher, uncovering her bare sex, and he almost lost it. She was smooth and perfect.

The throbbing in his dick no longer mattered. Besides,

he hadn't exactly brought condoms with him to the damn theater. But he had to have her, feel her, taste her.

He sank to his knees and kissed his way up her legs, opening them with gentle persistence. His thumbs massaged the crease between her legs, separating her thighs farther until he had enough access to slide through her wetness.

He tipped his head up to find her staring at him, her eyes hooded with need. "Lean into the wall, Vicks. Open wide. I want all of you on display for me."

She didn't question or even hesitate. It was as if all she'd needed was for someone—for him—to give her permission. Even in the dim light, it was obvious how slick her folds were. He wanted nothing more than to bury himself in her, to feel her squeezing his cock, but that could wait. Instead, he moved in, shifting his thumb to her clit while his tongue took its place.

She tasted like the world's sweetest nectar. His tongue probed inside her, and her hips tilted toward him, opening even more. Thrusting a finger into her, he swept his tongue over her folds, flicking on the nub of her clit. She tightened around his finger, but she was so wet, he knew she could take more—probably wanted more. So he eased in another and then another.

Her hips ground against his fingers and mouth as he thrust and sucked on her clit. Wetness ran down his hand, and her breathing became more ragged and desperate. One hand left her dress, and she twined her fingers in his hair, urging him on. Knowing how much she was enjoying it, he would have done this all night. But then her grip in his hair tightened and her insides squeezed his fingers, and he knew she was close.

He nibbled and sucked on her, his mouth and fingers pushing her closer and closer to the brink as the music from the orchestra swelled. The crescendo outside hit just as she cried out from the orgasm. She bucked against his fingers, riding out the waves until she was spent. Her legs trembled, and she sagged against the wall. Dante was sure she would have slid down to the floor if he hadn't helped keep her upright.

He allowed himself one last, lingering taste of her and then stood. With one arm around her waist to keep her standing, he used the other hand to straighten her dress. "Better?"

The smile that crossed her lips was dazed, her eyes more than a little glassy. "Amazing." Then she shifted and blinked down at his crotch. "But you…"

As painful as it would be to get through the rest of the fund-raiser, he'd realized while feasting on her that he never would have been satisfied with a quickie behind the curtain.

No. He wanted what she'd promised him that night at the party. He wanted her with him, in bed, all night long. Only this time, his would be the right bed instead of the wrong one. This time, she'd come because she wanted *him*, and he was more than willing to wait for that.

Easing her back through the curtain, he whispered through the golden halo of her hair, "I'm hoping this wasn't a one-time thing. I fully expect we'll be taking care of me later."

Twisting toward him, she covered his mouth with hers, her tongue tracing his lips, licking her own flavor from him. When they parted, her eyes were hooded with the kind of want that said she was ready to go again whenever he was. Then she reached toward him and rubbed her hand over the length of his erection. "Does this mean I'm special enough you want to show me your piercing?"

"Vicky, it means you're special enough I want you to feel my piercing in every position you can think of." And maybe a few that hadn't been invented yet.

. . .

For the remainder of the opera, the only thing Vicky could think about was getting Dante alone. Her walls weren't just cracking. They weren't even starting to crumble. They'd quite simply vanished. Or he'd jumped over them. Or... something.

All she knew was every reason she'd come up with to keep her distance was gone. Even sitting in separate seats felt like too much space between them. She wanted to touch him and never stop.

By the time the second standing ovation was over, she was grabbing his hand. "So...are we done here?"

"Soon." He ran a finger down her cheek and tucked her hair back. "Why do I get this sudden feeling we're not going out anymore?"

"What do you mean?" Her heart started to race. Was he saying it was over? He couldn't be saying that, could he? It made no sense.

Dante pulled her close, crushing her against a wall of muscle. "I'm saying that it seems like you're suddenly wanting to stay in rather than go out tonight. Feel free to correct me if I'm wrong."

Oh. That kind of not going out. "Staying in for a while sounds good. Really, really good."

Chuckling, he tipped her head back. "I'm sure we can work something out." He planted the softest kiss on her lips, and she immediately thought of his mouth somewhere else. The time between leaving their box at the opera and getting on their plane to go home was the longest of Vicky's life. Longer than waiting for the divorce to finalize. Longer than waiting for her first paycheck from Elegant Entertainment. Longer than going two years without sex.

She'd hoped to jump him in the limo, but they wound up sharing it with some other people on their way to the airport as well. By the time they boarded the plane, it was all she could do to let the pilot close the door and disappear into the cockpit before turning to Dante. "Mile-high club?"

Dante took her hand, turning it over to press his lips to the inside of her wrist and said, "Vicks, you have no idea how hard it is to say this, but no." When she opened her mouth to protest, he covered it with a finger. "I have wanted to be with you since I met you. I don't know how you felt back then, but I've never stopped wanting you. I finally get to have you, and I want it to be perfect. Even if it's the fulfillment of a fantasy, on a plane isn't good enough. You deserve the best, most romantic night I can give you. Will you let me do that?"

"I...I..." She wanted sex, and she wanted it now. The look in his eyes, though, told her this moment had the opportunity to mean more than stroking her screaming libido or completing her deal with Jade. Sleeping with Dante had the potential to be real. The thought alternated between terrifying and exhilarating, but every time she stopped to breathe, it landed on the latter. "Okay."

"Good." He leaned across the armrest and pressed his mouth to hers, the heat of the kiss finally making her give in to thinking of him as the Inferno. He could burn her up if he wanted, and she'd let him. "I have some calls to make. Why don't you take a nap so you'll be well rested by the time we get to my place?"

His place? He was taking her home? Sure, she'd see it eventually for party planning, but this was different. More. And from the sounds of it, she'd both need and want that rest he suggested. "Good idea. I'm just…going to use the restroom first."

He didn't say anything, likely realizing she never had gone at the opera, but her bladder wasn't the reason she needed it now, either. As soon as she had the tiny door latched behind her, she sagged against the door, desperate to control her seemingly unquenchable need for him. She'd come so hard at the opera, and he hadn't had any release yet. But now that she had him, she wanted more—she wanted him inside her in all the ways the opera hadn't allowed. She wanted to make him feel at least a fraction of what he'd given her. Inhaling and exhaling slowly, she mentally repeated her new mantra.

If he can wait, I can wait.
If he can wait, I can wait.
If he can wait, I can wait…

· · ·

"Yes, Ingrid, the delivery should be there within thirty minutes." Dante glanced over at Vicky. She'd insisted she wasn't tired, but about fifteen minutes later, her breathing evened out and he'd been able to make all the necessary arrangements. His housekeeper was both the first and now last call.

"Are you sure you don't need anything else? I could put supper on for you."

He didn't know why, exactly, but the idea of Vicky's first meal at his place being prepared by Ingrid was really bothersome. "No. That's not necessary. If you could grab the best bottle of pinot gris I have and chill it, though, that would be fantastic."

"Consider it done." She paused as he heard the doorbell in the background. "The delivery is here. Do you want me to take care of it or have them set everything up?" Dante could hear the distaste in her voice at the second option. Ingrid had very strong opinions about workers in the home. Namely, the fewer, the better.

"If you don't mind…"

"Not at all." He could almost see her puff up with pride.

"We're landing soon. I'll text when we're almost there."

"Everything will be just as you requested, and I'll sneak out like I was never here."

"Thank you, Ingrid." He thumbed off the phone.

Ingrid had started out as a once-every-other-week housekeeper years ago. Now, he didn't know how he'd keep his place up without her. There was no doubt in his mind that she would take care of everything.

Well, almost everything.

The aching bulge in his pants wasn't her domain. It would be Vicky's soon enough, but if he didn't let off some pressure, he was going to embarrass himself.

Quietly as possible, Dante made his way to the tiny bathroom and locked the door. Even unzipping his pants was torture, the zipper scraping gently against his engorged cock as he slid it down. For a second, his eyes rolled back as his balls shifted, then he sucked in a breath and wrapped a hand around his shaft. He needed to do this, if only to get his body to relax.

Leaning against the wall, he stroked and imagined the way Vicky had looked at the opera, how she'd stood wide and willing before him. How she'd moaned and wrapped her fingers in his hair. The moment when she'd started to buck against him and cried out as she came.

Dante could barely see straight between the images and the pain in his balls. What he really wanted was her in here with him. All it took was the thought of her mouth on him instead of his hand, and he came with so much force he saw stars.

Breathing hard, he was still bracing one hand against the wall when the intercom dinged and the pilot announced they were circling to land. It seemed he had finished just in time to zip up and get back to his seat next to the woman of his dreams.

The woman who was rapidly becoming his reality.

Chapter Eleven

By the time Dante unlocked the door of his Nantucket-style house, Vicky was shaking. Then she saw the rose petals on the floor. "Dante?"

He was grinning like the Cheshire cat. "Follow them. I'll be there in a second. I have something to grab first."

It didn't take more than a gentle nudge to get her moving. The petals were in shades from the palest pink she'd ever seen to a deep, dark red. They formed a carpet over the hardwood, straight up the stairs and around the landing to a slightly ajar door. Small motion-sensitive lights had come on as she moved, but the path now seemed to lead into the dark.

She cast a glance at the door, then back the way she'd come. Dante had said to follow the rose petals, but did he mean for her to go inside or wait here?

Soon enough, curiosity won out over caution. She pushed the door open and found herself bathed in candlelight. The flower path led straight to the massive bed, where a single red rose waited on a white pillow.

"Do you like it?"

Vicky gave a little jump as Dante's voice came from behind her. She hadn't heard him at all. "It's... Do you do this for all your women?"

A glass of wine entered her field of view as he wrapped an arm around her. She took it with trembling hands, and he whispered into her ear, "First, stop. There are no *all my women*. There's you. And, if it really matters, I've never done anything like this before."

The entire scene, it was too much. Combined with the stress and pent-up desire of the day, she giggled. "I feel like I've walked onto a movie set."

He nipped at her earlobe. "Is that a bad thing?"

"It's just every romantic cliché ever."

"Again...is that really a bad thing?" He trailed kisses down her neck, and her eyelids fluttered until she finally gave in and let them close.

"No. Just unnecessary. All I want is you."

Slowly, as if moving to some music she couldn't hear, Dante stepped around her, took both their wineglasses, and set them on his dresser. Then he wrapped her hands in his and led her toward the bed. "And I want you. But I also want you to feel like I give a damn." He picked up the red rose and handed it to her. "I want you, Vicky Stone. I've wanted you for five years, and I sure as hell want you to know I thought you were worth the wait."

The smile that crossed her face felt so unfamiliar she didn't recognize it at first. Then she remembered...the last time she'd worn it was the first time Dante had flirted with her—five years ago. It was shy and quiet and so unlike her normal personality that it seemed he was the only person in the entire world who could bring it out. She took the rose, unashamed of her response but trying desperately to redis-cover the woman who'd thought about jumping him on their flight, much less the one who'd let him eat her out at the opera. "Now what?"

"Now"—without warning, he swung her into his arms, and she let out a little shriek—"I ravage your body until you can't handle it anymore." The next thing she knew she was on the bed, his mouth on hers as her zipper slid down. His lips traveled lower as he eased the dress off her shoulder.

As soon as he found her nipple, he began teasing it with his tongue, and Vicky's eyes rolled back in her head. God, no one had done that for…years. Too many years. He sucked it firmly into his mouth, and she groaned, arching off the bed.

Dante took the opportunity to slide her dress the rest of the way off, releasing her breast in the process. Then he looked down at her with heat in his eyes. "If you'd asked me earlier if you could be more beautiful than you were at the opera, I would have insisted there was no way. But now… You are the most gorgeous view on the face of the planet."

Vicky ducked her head, blushing. Shy again. What was it about him that made her feel like such a teenager? "It'd be even better if we were naked and gorgeous together. Don't you have some new tattoos to show me or something?"

His lips shifted to his trademark grin, and her insides tightened, wishing there was something to clench. Then he yanked off his bow tie and lost his jacket and shirt. Jesus, she'd forgotten how perfect he was. Every inch of him chis-eled muscle, and on top of that art was the beautiful ink work he'd had done. Before he went for his pants, she sat up, her fingers tracing the new piece right below his clockwork heart. The script was simple, and in that simplicity was its beauty. It was nothing but the word "trust."

Dante didn't say anything as she examined the tattoo. It wasn't his only new piece, but it fascinated her, as if he needed a daily reminder to trust his own heart.

She pressed her lips to the ink, to the warmth of his skin, and then shifted her gaze to look up at him. "I trust you, Dante, more than you can possibly know." She did, too, and for the very first time, it didn't scare her at all.

• • •

A fist squeezed around Dante's heart. If she knew what the tattoo was really about, she might not trust him—at all. But they weren't here to talk about his past, much less relive things that had gone so very wrong. Tonight was about *this* moment and making sure it went right. Her fingers were still on the tattoo, and he grasped her wrist, shifting her hand away, and pulled her to stand in front of him. "Undo my pants. I want to feel you touching me like you did that first night, but this time I want you to know it's *me* you're touching. Know that I'm the one who is hard for you, aching for you."

"No wrong bed this time." Vicky's hand eased from his grip and slid down his skin to cup him through his pants. Her lips quirked to the side as he let out a low moan. This was torture, but it was worth it. As if she wanted to make his agony last, she slid the zipper down as slowly as possible. "I like that sound. Make it for me again."

He couldn't have resisted if he tried. He moaned, louder and longer, as her fingers slid beneath the silk of his trousers. A slight shift of her hands, and his pants dropped to his ankles.

"How did I know you were the kind of guy to go commando?"

Dante had to clench his teeth for a second as her grip tightened and she stroked him. When he was sure he could breathe again, he laughed, saying, "I've been told a gentleman always dresses to match his lady."

"Smart-ass." She stroked him again, fingering his tip, and he hissed in a breath. "What happened to the piercing?"

If he didn't have her soon, he was going to explode. As it was, he could barely focus on the question. "Some people worry about piercings and condoms, so I took it out until we could both get tested and I could confirm you were on birth control, too, just in case."

Her ministrations paused for a moment, and she said, "That's incredibly thoughtful of you. So thoughtful, in fact, it makes me want to give you something, too."

Before he formed a thought to respond, she was on her knees and wrapping her lips around him. Her warm, wet mouth stroked him, sucking all the while. His hands tangled in her hair, moving with her, until the moment his balls started to go tight. No. This wasn't what he'd planned at all, no matter how fucking fantastic it felt. Using his hold on her hair, he gently drew her off his cock. "Vicks, not tonight. I want to be buried hilt-deep between your legs the first time I come with you. And maybe the second and third, too."

The smile that shone up at him was full of something that looked so much like love it made his heart ache again.

"I'd like you buried hilt-deep in me as often as possible."

He almost came on the spot. "Lie down."

With a condom in hand, Dante crawled on the bed after her. If he rolled it on now, things would be over far too soon. Better to make sure they were both well satisfied.

He lay on his side next to her and toyed with her nipples. "I'm going to touch you, and I want you to tell me when you like what I'm doing."

"And on the off chance I don't?"

"Then show me how to do it better." Her laugh was cut off when his fingers slid between her legs, sweeping wetness over her labia. His touch glided over her skin even as he put pressure on her clit. She was so damned hot and wet, her skin soft as silk. "Like this?"

"Yes," she gasped. "But rub it."

Dante smiled against her breast, nipping at the curve. He loved the way she sounded, breathless and so incredibly turned on. He was going to milk this moment for all he was worth. "Rub it how?"

Her hips started to shift against his hand, and she whimpered. "Circles, back and forth, I don't care, just please…"

As if she knew he'd do anything with that one word attached to it, she didn't bother finishing the sentence. His fingers moved in slow circles over her clit, and he watched as her eyes rolled back.

"More, Dante. I need more."

"You want me inside you?"

"Yes. So fucking much."

He was so hard he was afraid even with jacking off on the plane that he'd come as soon as he entered her. But he also knew it would be like this until he finally had her, at least once. He eased his fingers into her cleft. Hot and soaked, she clenched at him as she moaned her need again. Thank God. Inside her, even like this, he wasn't sure he could wait any longer. He had the condom on in seconds and poised himself over her, his cock teasing her entrance.

She looked up at him, desperation in her eyes as she pleaded, "Are you trying to kill me?"

Only as much as he was trying to kill himself with waiting. "I just wanted to make sure you knew how beautiful and amazing I think you are."

"I know. Just please f—"

Her breath caught as he thrust into her and her muscles clamped around his length. He held still for a minute, just enjoying the sensation of her grip—on his dick, on his arms. "Sorry. If I went any slower, it'd be over already."

Reaching up, she twined her fingers in the ends of his hair. "Never, ever, *ever* apologize for doing what you just did to me."

He lowered himself to plant one soft kiss on her lips. "Message received, loud and clear." Pushing up, he grinned at her, watching as that shyness made her lower her lashes. "And with that in mind, you better hold on."

If she didn't want him to hold back, he sure as hell wasn't going to restrain himself. He'd waited too long for this moment. From the first thrust, every move he made, her body responded, curving toward his, her muscles flexing, pushing them closer. It was as if their very skin wanted to merge. She went from clinging to his biceps to her fingernails digging into his pecs, the little points of pain driving him on but making it harder and harder to delay his orgasm.

She clenched around him, and her mouth dropped open.

It might have been the force of her orgasm. It might have been the sound of her screaming his name. Or the way it echoed in the empty house. Whatever the ultimate cause, he came with so much force his arms shook as he held himself over her.

It wasn't until the muscles of her vagina relaxed that he pulled out. Lying next to her, he drew her close until her head rested on his chest, right over his heart. "That was worth the wait."

"I'm not so sure." He opened his mouth to retort, but she nipped at his chest and said, "I'm kind of kicking myself for making you wait at all."

He was, too, but he certainly wasn't going to bring up her ex. Not now, not ever if he didn't have to. "We definitely need to make up for lost time. It might take me a few minutes to recover, though."

"Maybe we could find other ways to entertain ourselves." She lazily traced his ink with her fingernail, and he tried not to shiver beneath her.

"What did you have in mind?" As long as it involved the two of them naked and together, he was in.

"Well, I do have one idea that could be kind of hot…"

• • •

Vicky bit her lip. She'd read about this a couple times; she'd just never thought to actually *do* it. But with all the candles burning around them, how could she resist? "Are your eyes closed?"

"How many times are you going to ask me that, Vicks?"

"Until I believe you?" But she looked at the *trust* tattoo

on his chest and realized she'd believed him the first time. She was afraid once she started that he'd freak and think less of her. Which was stupid. The guy had tattoos all over and had pierced his magnificent dick. A little hot wax wasn't going to bother him.

She picked up the nearest candle, a thin burgundy taper, and held it far away from his chest. He hissed in a breath as the first drop hit.

"Too hot?" She winced.

"No. I wasn't expecting it, is all." He wiggled a little beneath her, seeming to get more settled against the mattress. Definitely not bothered.

Vicky let out a breath, her nerves leaving with it. Dante wasn't Brandon. Dante honestly wasn't like any guy she'd ever been with. He trusted her as much as she trusted him. The feeling made her bold, and she tipped the candle, trailing wax all over the side of his chest free of ink. "I want to put my art on you, too."

His pecs twitched. "You can mark me however you want."

"In that case, I want more color." She returned the taper to its holder and picked up a little magenta votive and drizzled wax in a heart shape as Dante tensed his muscles beneath hers. A little longer, and all she was going to want to do was claw her nails through the wax and do whatever was necessary to get him ready to take her again.

She put the votive back on the shelf over the bed and grabbed a bold red pillar. There was a nice puddle of melted wax just begging to decorate him. If she was careful, maybe she could use it to fill in the heart she'd just drawn. Lowering it for more control, she tilted it sideways.

Had Vicky not been sitting astride him, Dante would have been off the bed with the way his body jumped. "Son of a bitch!" The candle went flying, thankfully extinguished by the rush of air against it.

Vicky rolled off him. "Oh my God. Are you okay?"

"Yeah," he moaned. Wincing, he tried to lie still. "No," he said as he got up.

She made it to the bathroom before he did, dousing a washcloth in cold water. She pressed it to his skin as he stepped into the brightly lit room, and his eyes rolled back so quickly she worried he might pass out. "Dante?"

"I'm still here. Not sure all my skin is, though."

A quick peek under the washcloth showed the flesh right around the last of the wax almost matched it in color. "I'm so sorry."

"Don't." He caught her hand and held on until she met his eyes. "I was enjoying it until that. Don't get the look that says *never again*. We'll buy some low-temp candles. You know, the kind designed for this sort of thing."

"I burned you, and your reaction is 'we'll just do it better next time'?" He shrugged, and she shook her head, wondering why the hell she'd been avoiding him for so damn long. "What are you? Superhuman?"

"Nah. I just really like you." He leaned in and planted a soft kiss on her forehead. "Okay, I think it's cooled enough to flake it off."

Vicky's hand hovered over the wax, fearful again. "What if it's burned really badly? Shouldn't we take you to a doctor?"

"I've survived a lot worse than a wax burn, Vicks. Though you might owe me after this."

As much as she tried *not* to think about what she would owe him, as Vicky peeled the wax from his very red skin, she found herself imagining all sorts of options, each one getting her more and more excited—making her more and more wet. When the last flake of wax was gone, she pressed her lips to his tender flesh, trailing kisses over every inch she'd burned. "I *am* really sorry. How can I make it up to you?"

He twisted his fingers in her hair, drawing her head back and pulling her body close with his other hand. No matter how badly his chest might hurt right now, other parts of him were functioning perfectly fine, especially the one getting harder and harder against her abdomen. "You can start by heading back into the bedroom. You're on top this time—I want you to show me exactly how sorry you are. And I want to see every inch of you while you're busy apologizing."

"I'm *very* sorry. This apology could take a while. Maybe all night." She could barely restrain her smile as she stepped into the candlelit glow of the master bedroom.

Dante was right behind her, his presence like heat at her back, warming her straight to her core. "I'm counting on it."

Chapter Twelve

Today was the day. The cast had to attend a mixer for the makeup line that was going to be launched to go with the movie. Which meant Reed would be in attendance. Dante thought about telling Vicky she could skip this one. But he wasn't going to be able to keep her away from Reed forever. Not to mention, how was he supposed to keep a woman away from a party where they'd be giving out free makeup?

"Are you sure I'm dressed okay? I never did this sort of party with Evan." Vicky smoothed down the skirt with her hands.

"Positive. And stop being so nervous. You never went with your brother because he was your brother." Dante took her fingers and gave them a squeeze.

"And what am I to you?" When he looked askance at her, she shrugged. "I didn't want to bring it up, but I really don't know. You're my brother's best friend, an Elegant Entertainment client, the guy who blackmailed me to go out with him…but now? We had sex—a lot of sex over the last two days. I mean, we even went and got STD tested together, which I don't think normal people *do*. Are we more than what all that other stuff says about us or not?"

It was a fair question, more than fair, really, but he didn't want to chase her away with labels. She'd made it pretty clear that she'd been looking for something casual initially, and sex didn't mean that had necessarily changed. "What do you want us to be?"

"Dante…" Every ounce of exasperation came out as she sighed his name.

"I'm serious." What he also was, though, was avoiding any talk of the blackmail—especially in lieu of them seeing Reed soon. He wanted to come clean, but not with that ass around, not if there was any chance Vicky was still interested. "I don't want to smother you, but I don't want to scare you off, either. So I'll ask again, what do *you* want us to be?"

She opened and closed her mouth a few times as if she wasn't sure what outcome she'd hoped for or expected. This time her sigh was just as heavy, only with sadness tingeing it now. "I guess we can't be anything other than friends officially. You're a client, which means the same rules as before apply anyway. At least as far as the general public is concerned."

Dante pulled the car to a stop and arched a brow at her. "You mean if we fall madly in love, get married, and have two-point-five kids, you won't be able to be my party planner anymore?"

"I…don't know." Vicky's brows knit together, and she started chewing on her lip. "That might be an exception, but I can also see Mathew insisting you work with someone else."

Huffing out a breath, Dante climbed out from behind the wheel. He hadn't much liked her boss, but if the guy was *that* close-minded about relationships and work, Dante didn't relish the idea of sending more business his way. "That's stupid," he said as he opened Vicky's door and took her hand. "You'd be better off starting your own company."

"Sure. On my waitress salary and total lack of experience." When he opened his mouth, she covered it with her hand. "And don't even suggest taking a handout from my brother. This is *my* life. I'll fix it."

He was going to mention finding an investor, not a handout, but it was clear she didn't want to discuss it at all, so he pressed a kiss to her palm instead. "Wouldn't think of it." Her hand drifted down, skating over his chest, and he winced.

She snatched her hand back. "I'm sorry. Does it still hurt?"

"Only a little. It's more the surprise of sudden contact there than a deep pain, if you know what I mean." He took her hand in his and led her to the door.

"I'm not positive, but I still feel like I didn't adequately make it up to you."

Thinking back to the sex right after their wax play and then how they'd spent most of the next day in bed, he couldn't agree with her, but he also wasn't going to disagree. "If you feel so strongly about it, you can apologize again when we get back to my place tonight."

"I'm spending so much time there now...are you sure you want me around this much?"

More. He wanted her around more. "If I start

complaining, you'll know it's time to leave." The instant the door closed behind him, Dante grabbed her wrist and pulled her back into his arms. "I should warn you, though, I'm not a big fan of complaining."

"I'll keep that in mind." She spun out of his arms, and they made their way through the tables. It was interesting to watch her in an atmosphere like this when she'd been on the staffing side of it only last week. She was much more polite to the servers than most people, always saying thank you and taking care to move out of their way rather than expecting them to shift around her. They seemed such little things, but Dante noticed most others treated the staff like background noise. Not that anyone was rude; they just skipped the niceties. Vicky didn't.

Whether she realized it or not, her working for Elegant Entertainment was kind of like working at the diner for him—it affected how she saw people from there on out. While Dante had always noticed waitstaff at restaurants, this was different. These people didn't have to be friendly as a way to get better tips, but they responded so much to how Vicky acted with them, making a point of smiling at her and bringing new dishes by them first.

It was strange how he'd never thought about all the other people who helped him in small and big ways since he'd come to L.A. He'd always just focused on the diner since moving, and Lee Corbitt before that. He rubbed at his shoulder, remembering again, part of him still wishing he could forget, could forgive himself. Ever since he'd let Vicky into his life, the old injury had been aching, like a physical reminder that he hadn't really opened up to her, not in the way he tried to delude himself into believing he had.

They'd been at the party a couple hours when he first caught sight of Reed. The asshole was *obviously* drunk off his ass, crashing into people and tables. Whether he'd shown up that way or taken too much advantage of the open bar didn't matter. What did was that it helped Dante get Vicky out of here before the two of them ran into each other.

He managed to lure her away from the display showing the new line that would debut with the film, and they were almost to the door when Saul called his name. *Damn it.* Ten more feet and they'd have been home free.

He turned, plastering a smile on his face. "Hey, Saul."

"Planning to leave without saying hello?" The producer's brows drew together as he glanced at Vicky.

"Just planning to leave before a food or fistfight broke out." Dante didn't bother gesturing toward Reed. He didn't have to; Saul knew exactly who he meant.

"Probably for the best." He was still staring at Vicky when he shook his head. "I'm sorry. I swear we've met before, but I can't place you. And trust me when I say I'm usually very good at remembering beautiful young actresses."

Vicky's cheeks flushed crimson. "I'm not an actress, but we met at your party last week."

"We did?"

Dante knew Saul would remember her eventually, so trying to pretend she wasn't the girl he'd caught sneaking out wouldn't do anyone any good. "Evan's sister, remember?"

"Oh." He blinked and looked her up and down—not a lecherous appraisal, more a respectful appreciation. "I'm sorry for not recognizing you sooner. You look lovely, my dear." He turned to Dante. "A word, please?"

Shit. The longer they were here, the more chance Reed

had of getting his hands on Vicky. Dante smiled at her. "Wait for me here? I'll be right back."

"How about I wait outside? If I stay near this rich food much longer, I'm going to eat so much I'll make myself sick."

Even better. "Sounds good." As soon as she was out the door, he turned to Saul. "What's up?"

"Is she your friend's sister or something more, Dante? I saw how you were looking at her…"

As much as Saul didn't want his cast mixing with staff, Dante trusted the guy to see this was a different sort of situation. "She's Evan's sister first and foremost, but we've been seeing more of each other since your party. I don't know where it's going, exactly, and she's nervous about what her boss will say if this gets back to him…" Especially since he'd forced the guy into a corner where the birthday party was concerned.

"I'm going to have a hard time keeping a lid on Reed if you're dating party staff."

"You're going to have a hard time with Reed no matter what I do. We both know that, Saul." Dante raked a hand through his hair. "She's not *staff*. I'm hanging out with my best friend's sister. If any questions come up, that's all you have to say."

Saul let out a harried sigh as a table behind them crashed to the floor. "I don't need any more bad publicity with this film, Dante. Please remember that."

"I always do." He was out the door seconds later, pondering how a romance they were both trying to keep under wraps could possibly lead to any publicity—good or bad. Then he heard Reed yelling from inside and realized they weren't the only players in the game. Where Reed was around, bad press was almost guaranteed.

. . .

Dante had to go to the studio for an official movie meeting, and Vicky was on her own for the first time in what felt like forever. She was also at his place, which felt so wrong she wasn't sure how to handle it. He'd left first thing in the morning, so she'd started with a shower.

Even hunting through the kitchen to find the bowls and some cereal felt like an intrusion. As if peeking behind the white-glazed hardwood doors was somehow invading his sacred space. And now, with the dishes loaded in the dishwasher, she couldn't figure out what to do with herself. The debate over leaving didn't last long. He'd be home in a couple hours and they were supposed to do some party planning and then take a long swim in his pool.

No. She needed to stay, which meant she needed to figure out a distraction.

With a bowl of grapes and a glass of water to keep her company, she set her laptop and binder on the bar and took a seat. The tentative guest list was the first thing in her files, and she realized now was the perfect time for the task she'd been avoiding. It was shortly after noon in Detroit, which meant it was time to call Evan.

Vicky bit her lip and pulled up his number. It rang a full three times, and she was readying for it to go to voicemail when her brother came on the line, breathless. "Hey, Vicky. Long time, no hear."

Had it been? She tried to remember the last time she'd called. It had been before she ran into Dante, probably close to a week before. She hadn't called Mom in that long, either. Oops. "Life got a little crazy out here."

"Tell me about it."

That sounded like the beginning of a bad joke. He'd tell her to get the hell away from Dante, and now that they'd had sex, she wasn't willing to give him up that easily. "Well, I got a surprise temporary promotion."

"What the hell is a temporary promotion? And congrats, I guess?"

That might not have been the right way to go. "It's temporarily good. It'll give me some money to pocket away." She bit her lip for a second. There was no way to tell him about the party without mentioning *how* she'd gotten the promotion. "It's actually kind of funny. I was working a party and ran into Dante, of all people."

"Dante?" The shock in his voice was enough to make her speed through the rest.

"Well, he came up with this idea to throw a dual birthday party for the two of you and convinced my boss that I was the only one to handle it. Hence surprise temporary promotion. I need to talk to you about the guest list." She bit her lip, praying his reaction wasn't over-the-top.

"Vicky, what the hell were you thinking?"

Damn. "Career? Money? Getting my life on track?"

He laughed. "I meant more what were you thinking planning a birthday party for me when Stasia's pregnant and due in less than a month? Dante might not have realized the timing, but you knew."

Oh, God. She had forgotten completely. "I...I'm so sorry." What the hell was she going to do? Mathew would fire her when he found out she knew this party couldn't happen.

She had no choice, though; she had to cancel or at least postpone. Thank goodness she hadn't actually ordered anything yet. "I'll talk to Dante today, and we'll call it off."

A deep sigh echoed over the phone. "No. Stasia would have my head if I hurt your chances at moving up at Elegant. Email me what you have for a guest list so far and the rest of the details. I'll talk to her."

"Evan, you don't have to do that. This was my screwup."

"You know, it's kind of crazy, but the biggest thing I've learned this past year is that you'll do a lot for the people you love. Stasia might be a little torqued at me, but she'll be totally on board with helping you in the only way you'll let us." He paused, and Vicky realized she *was* letting people bail her out…again. Then he continued, "You kicked my ass last year with Stasia, Vicky. She knows that, and we *both* owe you. Without you, there'd be no baby on the way."

It still felt wrong, like she wasn't proving herself with the party. She was just proving who she knew, and who would do anything to build her up again.

And if that was the case, how was she supposed to be strong enough to stand when it all came crashing down around her again?

"But I need to do this on my own. I can't have everyone bailing me out all the time."

"Here's the thing, Vicky, everyone gets bailed out. Yes, learn to do as much as you can on your own because it's important to not run to people looking for them to fix your shit, but the only ones who have *no one* helping out are the ones who live alone and off the grid. You have family, you have friends, you have people who want you to be the best damn Vicky Stone you can be."

He didn't get it. "That's great, but you can't pick me up every time I trip and fall. Or I'll never learn."

"That's funny, because I remember teaching you to ride your bike. Mom or I picked you up every time—until you didn't need us to anymore. You still learned."

"It's not the same."

"Nope. It's bigger, because whether or not you learn to ride a bike is pretty unimportant in the grand scheme of life. People help me all the fucking time. You do. Mom does. Stasia sure as hell does. I don't go it alone unless I *have to*. That's the real secret—you need to be strong enough to do it when necessary but vulnerable enough to let others in. A wise person taught me that."

"Really? Who was that?"

"You, dumbass. Send me the party stuff, and I'll get back to you tomorrow. Meanwhile, get your head on straight before I send Mom out there to do it for you."

And that is the very last thing I need.

The part that frightened her the most was the realization that she had been on her own for the last year. She'd been doing all the things that made her life run—if not smoothly, at least without major hiccups. Was she ready to take a step toward opening herself up again? Could she let herself *need* another person without turning into who she used to be? Was she strong enough?

There was only one way to find out.

And he'd be home in another hour.

Chapter Thirteen

When Dante got home from the meeting, Vicky met him at the door. Her hand was already sliding under his shirt, fingers tripping over his abs before she even said, "I need you."

It sounded like the exact opposite of everything she'd been telling him about not needing anyone, but it totally fed into his own urge to be there for people he cared about. "Then you've got me."

He let her lead the way upstairs, but as soon as they were on level ground again, she spun around and started kissing him while she unbuttoned his shirt. The feel of her hands and lips made him blind to everything, and when she backed against a door, he opened it without a thought. They fumbled in the darkened room until she sank onto a mattress, pulling him down on top of her.

They rolled until he was on the bottom…and right next to the edge. Which was when it hit him. "Vicks, babe, wrong bed…again." Teasing, he nipped at her collarbone.

"There's no such thing as long as you're the one in it with me."

The words were like magic to him—everything he wanted to hear. Unfortunately, something was off in her voice as she said it. Not to mention the way she was desperately clawing at his belt, as if its presence personally offended her. "Vicky, what's the matter?"

"Nothing. Can't a girl just want to have sex?"

"Of course you can. I like it. But I also want us to be real with each other."

At that, her motions stopped. No more clawing, no more stroking, no more anything. "And are we real? Is this?"

That morning, he'd given her a good-bye kiss while she was still lying in the bed they'd had sex in half the night. She'd given him a sleepy "have a great day, I'll miss you," and then dozed off before he made it out of the room. He'd been gone five hours. What the hell had happened?

"I've never not been real with you. As for this…" He took her hand and slid it against the length of his erection. "If you meant sex, yeah, I'd say the way you get me going is pretty fucking real." Then he slid her hand up his chest until her palm was flat against the beating of his heart. "If you meant more, I want real. I always have."

She rolled off him, her body in the path of light carved by the open door, and clawed her fingers through her hair. "I don't know what's real anymore. I don't even know what I want. I thought I did, and then you showed up and turned everything upside down."

Clearly, she was hurting, and he really didn't know how to help. Lee Corbitt's voice started ringing in his head. *Stop complicating things. The bigger the question, the harder it is to come up with a solution. Break it down into manageable bits. That's how you fix big things, son.* As much as Dante really didn't want memories of Lee invading his time with Vicky, the guy had been onto something.

He dragged her fingers from her hair, placing tender kisses on the tip of each one. "Let's start with right now, this very moment. You said you wanted me, do you? And I don't mean big picture, I mean right now."

"Yes."

Good, because he didn't think he'd have been able to handle it had she said no. He could help with this little portion of whatever was plaguing her. Then they'd go from there. One step at a time. "Then let me get you naked and make you forget all those other things that are stressing you out. Let me make you think about nothing but this moment and how very real it is."

"Okay."

It wasn't exactly the kind of enthusiastic response he'd gotten used to the last few days, but at the moment, she wasn't the same Vicky, either. This wasn't the woman at the opera or the one with the candle wax. This Vicky needed to be treasured in a way that had nothing to do with rose petals and candlelight. What she needed couldn't be bought.

Dante stood and tugged her to her feet. His clothes didn't matter now. It'd be a while before they got around to taking them off. Instead, he eased her shirt over her head, trailing kisses from her collarbone and down her arm as he moved. Then he unzipped the simple skirt she wore and pulled it over her hips, letting his lips linger on the subtle swell of her abdomen. Before they were done, he planned to have his mouth on every inch of her skin.

His thumbs hooked under the edge of her panties, tracing the line along her hip bones, savoring the softness of her skin. Even when he dropped them to the floor, he resisted the urge to focus on sex. This wasn't about the destination. Today, they were going to savor the journey.

With the gentlest of pressure against her thigh, Dante made Vicky turn around, and his mouth blazed a path from her hip up to the strap of her bra. Rather than the deft, single-handed unhook, he spread his palms flat, caressing her shoulders, massaging some of the tension from her inch by inch. Then, one hook at a time, he undid her bra, holding onto the straps to ease it down her arms while never losing contact with her skin.

His lips found the back of her neck, and he kissed her until she sank against him. Only then did he release her bra and wrap his arms tight around her. She trembled, but she tilted her head, allowing him access to more of her—to all of her. Slowly, he worshipped her body. Not just her breasts or her sex. All of her. Her golden hair and flawless skin, the muscles that played against his every touch, the sweetness of her kiss.

And then the pressure of her nails digging into his arms and her desperate breaths. "Please, Dante…"

He wished he could give her everything she needed, but she'd only let him give her this. There was no way he could deny her. After allowing himself a few blissful moments to taste the parts that had escaped his earlier, innocent attentions, he slid his pants down his legs, rolled on a condom, and crawled onto the bed between her thighs.

He didn't know how long they'd been in the room, but

the sun had moved so it no longer shone on the bed, and he very much wanted to see her. Reaching toward the nightstand, he flicked on the tiny lamp. It barely cast a glow in the dim room, but it was enough. It lit her tan skin and made the subtle highlights in her hair shine. Dante swallowed hard. "You are the most beautiful woman I've ever known."

Before she had a chance to respond or even take a breath, he slid between her folds, savoring the way her body opened to let him enter but held him tight at the same time. They fit perfectly together, exactly how he'd always known they would. And now, with Vicky relaxed and throwing her head back in bliss as she moaned his name, he knew she was finally willing to let him in, to let him rescue her from her past, from her demons.

Maybe, if he let her, she'd be able to rescue him, too.

As he moved inside her, he leaned down close so their bodies pressed together, somehow making the act of sex even more personal, more intimate, and whispered in her ear, "You were right, Vicks. No more wrong beds. I want you in mine from now on."

• • •

Vicky's phone rang as she was putting the finishing touches on an order for the party. Between talking to Evan and dealing with vendors, it seemed like it had been going off nonstop this morning, but at least she was in a better place than she had been yesterday. She still wasn't *sure* she was in the right place for a relationship, but she was more certain than she had been even twenty-four hours before. "Vicky Stone."

"Pretty sure I knew who I was calling when I told Siri

to call that dumbass who is apparently standing me up. Granted, when she said 'do you mean Vicky?' I had to say yes, because she knew exactly who we were calling."

"Oh my God, Jade, I'm so sorry." Vicky glanced at the clock on her laptop. She was indeed very late for their weekly lunch. "Do you still have time to meet if I leave right now?"

The sigh on the other end was the kind of deep that called her stupid in at least three languages. "Of course. I'll head toward your place. Is that Thai joint open for lunch?"

"Uh... I'm not at home."

"Did you go into the office today? I thought you had an event to waitress tonight." Jade's car door slammed, the sound echoing over the phone.

Vicky glanced around Dante's home office. She was going to have to spill, but it would be better in person, not to mention, even after the incredible night with Dante, she could really use a good talk with Jade right about now. "Not exactly. I'm in Brentwood. Know any place good around here?"

"Are you kidding?" When silence hovered, Jade laughed. "I'll text you an address. See you soon."

With the order drawn up, Vicky sent the email and headed out to the pool, where Dante was studying his script. "Hey, I totally forgot about lunch with Jade. I'll be back in a few hours, if that's not a problem."

He lowered his sunglasses and cocked a brow at her, making her insides turn to mush. "I'm not your jailer, Vicks. Go see your friend. We have all night tonight to ourselves."

"Okay. See you in a while."

Before she made it two steps, he was in front of her,

arms around her waist. "Go to lunch doesn't mean you get to leave without a good-bye kiss." He covered her mouth with his, kissing her until she was dizzy and giggling.

"Got it. No more sneaking out pre-kiss." For good measure, she pressed her lips to his neck, nipping at the spot he liked. Her voice softened when she added, "And thanks again for not deciding I was nothing but a big basket of crazy yesterday. I'll try not to get weird like that again. Back soon."

"I don't know, I didn't mind so much," he said, winking at her before turning back to his work.

Truth was, she hadn't minded so much in the end, either.

Finding the address Jade had texted was fairly quick — also a Thai place, though arguably more expensive than the one near her apartment. It took a while longer to find parking and get inside, though. Her friend was already seated, sipping a cocktail and looking altogether proud of herself.

"So, Brentwood. Does that mean you and the Inferno got your heat on together? Did you create enough friction to start a fire? Did you—"

"Did you spend the entire drive coming up with as many puns as you could?" Vicky shook her head and motioned for another of whatever Jade was having. She was pretty sure before lunch was over, she'd need it.

"Actually, I did. Spill."

"Yes, the fire started." If she hadn't given Jade a death-stare, she was pretty sure a high five would have followed the announcement. "But it didn't go out like it was supposed to." She paused as the waiter delivered the drink, then said, "None of this happened like it was supposed to."

Jade toyed with her straw. "Well, I do remember how nervous you were about going back to the mansion to even talk to him. Clearly you needed an assist. It doesn't surprise me at all that things turned out different than they looked on paper."

It was time to come clean on the whole mess. Even after yesterday, she needed advice, and she wasn't going to get that without a heaping dose of honesty. "The first hiccup was the fact that I wasn't supposed to almost have sex with Dante at all. I'd stayed for someone else."

The announcement wasn't what Jade had expected. She stopped messing with her drink and her jaw dropped open for several seconds before she said, "I... Go on."

"Dante and Evan are friends. I met him back when I was engaged to Brandon. Evan told me to stay away because he was bad news, so I did. Then he was at the party that night, and—"

"Irrelevant. Who *did* you stick around for?"

It felt so stupid admitting she'd ended up with one Hollywood superstar while trying to pursue another. "Reed Russell. But then I ended up in Dante's room by mistake. Then, when we went back for my ID, he threatened to report me for my behavior if I didn't go out with him instead."

Jade let out a low whistle and shook her head. "I'm not even going to ask what you mean by behavior. Sweetheart, you dodged a massive bullet. Reed Russell is the worst thing to come out of this town since *Battlefield Earth*. Seriously— bad, bad, bad news. I never would have encouraged you to find a lay at that party if I'd had any idea it could possibly be him."

"What do you mean?"

"I mean he's the guy the tabloids tone things down about. The real stories are worse. He's still here because he's made bank and has enough money to throw around and keep victims quiet. So many people I know refuse to work with him because of the turmoil he causes everywhere he goes. I even heard rumors about that party you worked. Supposedly he was caught with a teenage hooker or something. The guy is a force of nature—the really destructive kind. Blackmail or not, Dante did you a favor."

She'd wondered, more than once. The blackmail hadn't meshed with the guy she'd gotten to know, but why hadn't he come clean about it since then? She'd had sex with him, for God's sake—a lot of sex. Obviously, they'd moved beyond his threat to something more, and not just in her mind. "Okay, so...no Reed. I was over that anyway. The only reason I was even looking at him was I figured he'd be an easy one-and-done."

"Yeah, except he supposedly has the gift that keeps on giving, so 'done' is kind of the wrong word."

Definite bullet dodged. "Moving on. Far, far away from that. Like galaxies away..." Then there was Dante. While they ate, she told Jade everything: from the awkward first date to the party planning to the sex to the past couple days. "After we went to that makeup thing, he decided he didn't need to hit all the promo stuff, or at the very least that I didn't need to hit the events with him. The change of heart is weird, and then, after the hours and hours of sensitive sex yesterday, I don't know what to do with it. I don't know if the whole avoiding events means he's bored with me and looking to move on, or if the sweetness and attention at home means he's just wanting to keep me to himself, or what."

"Sorry, I'm still stuck on the piercing. Have you tried it yet?"

The piercing? In all that, Jade had focused on the piercing? "No. Test results should be back today, though, and I'm on birth control, so *if* things are solid, we'll go there soon."

"Damn. You'll definitely have to fill me in—sounds hot. Anyway, the issue…if he was going to everything and leaving you home, I'd say there was a worry, but it sounds like he wants you for himself. The more you're publicly out together, the more risk it'll get back to that douche bag boss of yours, so he's probably thinking this is what's in your best interest, at least until the party's done and you collect your big payday."

That was true. There were only a few things he was attending solo, but… "I'm scared, Jade."

"Of what?"

"This was supposed to be just sex. Well, blackmail and then just sex, but my rule about not getting involved with a guy…I'm breaking it. I care about him. I care about him a lot."

Jade sucked in a deep breath and pushed back from the table. "I don't do relationships, you know that. But you do. You're a believer in soul mates and happily ever after. It's a beautiful thing, and I'm honestly kind of jealous, but there's one problem with that way of thinking."

"Which is?"

"Life doesn't follow the logical ups and downs of the movies. Life likes taking sharp turns and switchbacks." When Vicky frowned, Jade reached out and squeezed her hand. "There's a thing about broken bones, that when they heal, they're stronger. Let me put it as simply as I can. You weren't going to be able to stick to your no-man plan forever because it's not in your nature. Your heart was broken, but it's not anymore. Could it be again? Of course, but it's stronger now. That stupid rule that was blocking your life from being what's normal for you? It needed to break sooner or later so that you can build something stronger there, too."

It made sense in the way that only Jade's weirdness could make sense. "And you think this thing with Dante is something stronger?"

"I think the only way you're going to find out is if you stop worrying at it and give it a chance." She tipped back what was left of her drink. "On the upside, he's the Inferno— he's more likely to burn you to ashes than actually break you."

It was supposed to be funny, but the only thing Vicky knew that rose from ashes was a phoenix, and she didn't think this was that kind of fairy tale.

Chapter Fourteen

Vicky had just sent the last of the emails to vendors when Dante suggested going to the gym. While it wasn't a fancy dinner out or a trip to the opera, it was a chance for her to see him outside of the Hollywood machine…more or less. Of course, she'd thought he meant his home gym until they were loaded in his car and headed out.

The place he stopped didn't have any big sign advertising its existence, and from the outside it looked like a warehouse. She frowned at him. "Did you bring me here to kill me?"

Dante laughed, the sound full and light. "Only if your heart is in much worse shape than marathon sex would suggest." He held the door open for her, and the sounds of grunting and metal clanking against metal met her ears. "I have a membership at a public gym, too, but this place is more exclusive—and quieter."

Inside, she saw a full array of cardio equipment, a massive range of free weights, and a few machines. As well as a roped-off ring surrounded by both speed and heavy bags. Dante swiped a card, and they walked through a security gate. "Nice place."

"Yeah, well, even superheroes have to stay in shape somehow, and here it's all industry people, so no one oohs and ahhs over one another." He took her bag and tossed it on a bench in the corner. "Also nice because no one messes with your shit. Treadmill or elliptical?"

Vicky stared at the options. She liked the workout better on an elliptical. But those were closer to everyone else in the gym at the moment, and what she really wanted was time alone with Dante in an atmosphere where he was comfortable enough to talk. This gym seemed like a perfect fit. "Let's do treadmill, but I'm a walk or jog girl. If you want speed, you're going solo."

"Jogging is fine."

A few minutes later, they were on the machines, moving at a pace not far beyond a fast walk. Perfect for working out while maintaining a minimal amount of conversation. She'd pondered so many times how to begin this chat, and decided to start on what seemed safe territory. Not too prying. "So, I've been meaning to ask you about the new ink…"

"What about it?"

"Why 'trust'?"

Dante reached over and adjusted her speed. "You're obviously not working hard enough."

As soon as he cranked up his own, she turned hers back down. "I said no running. I'm serious. Of all the words in the English language, why that one?" When he just kept running, she shook her head and turned toward the machine's display instead. Obviously, his walls were still firmly in place no matter what had happened to hers. "Never mind. Sorry I asked."

They finished their warm-up on the treadmill, and as Dante's machine stopped and he rolled off the back to land on his feet, he kept his hands on the rails, leaning into them. "I'm sorry. I wasn't expecting to talk about this right now."

"It's fine." It wasn't, but she could pretend it was. "I let it go."

"But you shouldn't have to." He toweled off his face and waved her toward the hand weights. While she selected a set for some curls, he said, "Remember the guy I told you about? Lee Corbitt?"

"Yeah. The one who saved you from a life of gangs and trained you to fight."

"The tattoo is for him. One of the first things he taught me was to trust my gut, my heart, and my head, in that order. He said my gut knew the truth, my heart knew what I wanted, and my head knew facts. All three agreeing on something was rare, but that when they did, it shouldn't be ignored."

Vicky made a face as she curled the weights. They were a little heavier than she should have gone. "He's a wise man."

"Was."

The way he said the word left no question as to what he meant, but he elaborated anyway. "I was on my way out of town for a match early in my wrestling career. He called to wish me luck. My gut told me something was wrong—his voice sounded off. Lee said a car had been driving by his place a lot, but that it was probably just his paranoia setting in. My heart said he might be right, but that someone should probably keep an eye out for him. At that point, he was getting older, and all his old wounds were wreaking havoc on him. I offered to stay home. He insisted I not worry so much, and it was what my head wanted to hear. The match was worth a decent chunk of change, and it had the potential to solidify my career."

"So you left."

"I left." Dante rubbed at his left shoulder as if it ached, even though he hadn't even picked up a set of weights yet. "That night, someone broke into his house and killed him. They stole a bunch of shit, too, but Lee didn't put much value in *stuff*. The people who did it were after him, not money." His eyes got a faraway look in them, one filled with pain and remorse. "You see, I wasn't the only kid he'd helped over the years, and Lee had never had any fear of the gangs. He'd report anything and everything to the cops. Someone decided they'd had enough."

"Dante…"

"Had I trusted my heart that night, he might still be alive, but I didn't. I trusted my head that told me to go for the payout."

It no longer mattered that they were in a gym, much less who might be watching. Vicky wrapped her arms around him and held him close. "It wasn't your fault."

"Maybe not, but it felt like it was." He sighed into her hair. "The Inferno was born after that. I sought out fights with guys who had been in gangs or who had reputations for anything bad. It didn't matter if we were supposed to be on the same side or not. I wanted to punish *someone* for Lee's death."

The reports about Dante's aggression and violence in the ring came back to Vicky then. She had her bit of truth about him, and she wasn't sure if she wanted to hold it tight or give it back.

Dante wasn't done talking, though. "I ran into one of the guys who'd originally tried to recruit me into the gang a couple years later. He made some smart-ass comment about 'old man Corbitt' and I lost it. I beat him bloody, and he put a knife in my shoulder. We both ended up in the hospital."

There'd been no police report. She would have found it if there had been. Obviously neither of them had pressed charges. "Is that what ended your wrestling career? The injury?"

"No. I could have gone back to it once I healed up, but the fight changed me. I realized I was becoming the very thing Lee had tried to keep me from turning into. If I stayed on that path, my whole avenging-angel wrestling persona could have turned into something much more violent, much more real. I would have wound up behind bars trying to right the wrong of his death. And he never would have forgiven me for that. So, at the height of my career, I left it all behind. The ink was a long time coming."

With the way he leaned into her, letting her support him, she had a feeling sharing the story had been a long time coming, too.

• • •

He'd done it.

Dante had managed to tell Vicky about the worst parts of his life…and she was still here. Now that they were home from the gym—working out had proved rather fruitless, but the trip was still worth it—he needed to know that she was staying.

Unfortunately, she was glued to her phone as they walked into the house. He couldn't help but wonder what had her so intent. Then she turned to him with a coy smile. "Dr. Blaise left a message, if you'd like to hear it. I'm all clear."

Which meant he should have a message, too. He keyed it up on his phone and put it on speaker. "Tests all came back negative. Let me know if there's anything else you need."

Vicky bit her lip as she looked at him. "So, does this mean we can leave the piercing in while we go cool off in the pool?"

This wasn't the conversation he'd expected—it was better. "Yeah."

"And does it mean we can leave it in *after* the pool?"

"Of course."

"And does it mean—"

"It means last one in the pool cooks dinner." He started toeing off his sneakers.

"Suits?"

"I have a privacy fence, and they wouldn't stay on long anyway."

"In that case…" Vicky had taken her shoes off at the door and now sprinted to the back, jumping in the water fully clothed.

He was still wearing his boxer briefs when he followed her out. "What was that all about?"

"I really hate cooking." Item after item of waterlogged workout wear splashed onto the deck, and he stood there, watching, until she was naked. "Are you coming in or what?"

"Sorry. Just enjoying the show." He discarded his underwear and dived into the water, coming up next to her and sweeping her into a kiss. "So, about that piercing…"

She wrapped her hand around him, stroking him gently under the water. Every time she came to his head, she toyed with the metal, making his toes curl. "I believe you promised me every position."

"That I did." He closed his eyes, savoring the feel of her touch. Reveling in the knowledge that no matter how far she'd run from him five years ago, this time she was staying. And for once, his gut, heart, and head all agreed on something: being with her was right. No, better than right. Being with Vicky was perfect.

Her lips trailed kisses from his shoulder up his neck. "Which one do we get to try out first?"

"I was thinking we'd come over here." Loath as he was to have her stop stroking him, he wanted to be inside her more, and he led her to the steps at the shallow end of the pool, where he sat down. "Then I was thinking you could sit on my lap."

· · ·

"And tell you what I want for Christmas? Isn't it a little early for that?" Contrary to her words, she straddled him, biting her lip when the balls of his piercing pressed on the front and back of her opening as she sank onto his head. Slowly, ever so slowly, she lowered her body, savoring the feel of the extra points of contact. Her eyes rolled back as the beads rubbed against her insides in ways she'd never felt before. "Oh, Santa, how did you know that was exactly what I wanted?"

Dante growled against her breast. "I will give you

anything you ever want, but I am not a big, fat man with a white beard."

She gasped as she sheathed him fully, her fingers digging into his biceps as his piercing rubbed against her walls. "And here I thought you were the new and improved sexy Santa. My mistake."

"Woman…"

"Shh…" She laid a finger over his lips as she lifted her hips, sliding off him. Never in her life had she experienced anything like this. The strange sensations had her muscles clamping down on him with every little movement. "It's really hard to concentrate on how amazing you feel when you keep talking."

He must have realized she was enjoying herself, and he shut up. Hands resting firmly on her hips, he guided her motions as she rocked, which was a good thing since reasonable thought was quickly vanishing as the combination of his dick and those two metal balls worked their magic, every move pushing her closer to the edge. The cold water around them did nothing to quench the heat they were building together.

Every time he plunged into her, she got tighter and tighter, clenching his length. "God, you feel so good. I didn't think you could feel better than before, but please don't ever take the piercing out again." She moaned loudly into his hair, her fists wrapped tightly in its length as she rode him, struggling to hold back from the rapidly building orgasm.

"As you wish." He held her just above the level of the water and shifted his weight so he could thrust into her—hard and steady. Water from her hair streamed over her breasts and down her abs to splash against his skin. If she locked her vision on that, she could almost control…

Then one of the balls hit her G-spot, and Dante must have noticed some change in her, because he became relentless. Over and over, he thrust to touch her there, and no amount of focus could restrain her any longer. Vicky's grip tightened, and she flung her head back. There was nothing but the feel of him inside her as wave after wave crashed. Her muscles would contract only to have his piercing rub against them and bring on fresh heat. Her breathing quickened with each new spasm, and Dante increased the speed and depth of his thrusts until they were both crying each other's names, their voices echoing in the still air.

Vicky let herself fall against his chest, settling there in the safety of his arms. This. She finally understood—this was right where she needed to be. Maybe the heroines in all the movies weren't damsels in distress after all. Maybe they were just women who'd figured out that the hero would, always and forever, do right by them. Even though she'd sworn against it, forever was starting to sound pretty good from where Vicky was sitting.

Chapter Fifteen

For almost two weeks, Dante had gone to events solo, but he'd skipped many of them entirely. Vicky wanted to believe Jade was right, but everything about it still felt wrong. It felt like the blackmail had—completely out of sync with Dante's personality. He was a personable guy. Chatting with people—friends or strangers—was when he seemed most in his element. That was when his stress seemed to melt away.

So when he brought up the cast dinner, Vicky decided it was time to put her foot down. "How fancy is this thing? Like wear the same dress as I did to the opera fancy? Cocktail dress fancy? Jeans and cowboy boots?"

"Oh," he said, avoiding eye contact, "you don't have to go. It's going to be mostly shop talk. You'd probably be bored to tears."

That was it. "You get that my brother's an actor, too, right? You understand that I'm not new to this whole scene? I may not be an industry insider, but I'm not an idiot, either.

What gives? Are we done, and I just didn't get the memo?"

"What? No. Of course not."

"Did Saul throw a fit because of me waitressing at his party?"

"No…"

"Then what is it? Because while I don't mind doing the whole just-old-friends thing because of my job, I'm starting to feel like I'm your dirty little secret." She slapped the party binder on the table. "And if that's the case, the job's done. Invites were sent a week ago. Most of the RSVPs are recorded. I can get out of your hair and finish up from my office."

"Damn it, Vicks, that's not it at all." Dante shoved the binder aside, sat on the edge of the table, and took her hands. "I'm going to come clean to you. Thing is, Reed's still in the movie. He's going to be at the dinner."

"And?" This was about *Reed*? She wasn't with him. Hell, she'd barely thought about him since things with her and Dante had started moving. The guy had been a means to an end, nothing more, and she'd already met that end in a much more pleasurable fashion.

"And I told you what he does to people. If he remembers you…"

"Seriously? *Saul* didn't remember me, and he caught me after hours with you. It's been weeks. I'm sure Reed Russell has forgotten all about the waitress-who-didn't-show by now."

"If you're wrong?"

Conversations like this made her wonder if people really did think she was helpless. She *had* made it through life before men started taking care of her. Granted, Mom had done most of the caretaking before that, but still, she was a strong, capable woman, damn it. It was high time people started treating her like one, even if she'd just figured it out herself. "I'm a big girl, Dante. I don't need you to play hero for me—whether to keep me away from danger or rescue me from it. If I'm wrong, *I'll* deal with Reed Russell and the Ego-that-ate-Frisco."

Dante leaned down and kissed her, hard, teasing her lips open with his tongue until she yielded to him. It was totally okay with her if they argued…as long as it always ended like this. He pulled back, planted another soft kiss on her forehead, and said, "In that case, cocktail dress."

The food was great—on that basis alone, she was glad she'd insisted on joining him. Otherwise, he hadn't been lying. Dinner was a giant snoozefest. The cast spoke about filming and motivation and blah, blah, blah while the spouses chatted about spa days, golf outings, and dinner parties. Vicky spent a lot of time toying with her phone.

Granted, she did listen in on the conversations about parties. If she really wanted to be a full-time planner eventually, any information was good information. By the time dessert came, she'd learned more about menu preferences and stupid expenses than she'd been able to type into the notes on her phone. There were *so* many ways Elegant Entertainment was wasting money that it almost made her head spin. Mathew probably wouldn't want to hear any of it, but if Vicky could continue to pay attention to this sort of thing, maybe when she finally had enough saved to break out on her own, she'd be able to set herself apart from the rest of the party planners out there.

Still, she would have been bored out of her mind if not for the way Dante kept his hand on her thigh all through the meal. At first she'd worried someone would notice, but everyone seemed to have their attention locked in on conversation. Everyone but Dante.

"I think it's important that we really drive home the fact that Andrew is a man first and a superhero a distant second. His identity is as a father, not a masked man—that's the guy the audience will relate to." Dante never hesitated as he spoke, but all the while, his fingers were tracing patterns on her skin until it was all Vicky could do not to jump him right then and there.

Until Reed spoke, and her entire body went on high alert. "I think you're overestimating our target audience. People come to these movies for muscles and explosions. No one gives a rat's ass about the hero's relationship with his twelve-year-old kid."

As much as she didn't want to draw Reed's attention, considering she'd avoided it so far, Vicky couldn't keep her mouth shut. She'd been a movie star's sibling too long. "And if you continually target nothing but the lowest common denominator of moviegoer, the franchise will die a slow, comedic death. Character depth keeps people coming back—explosions don't."

Reed glanced her way, but there was no recognition in his gaze. "Maybe you should leave the commentary to the professionals. Your job is just to sit there and look pretty."

The comment made Vicky bristle, but the patterns on her thigh had stopped being random. Over and over, Dante was drawing a heart on her skin until she finally turned her attention to him. "Don't let him get to you, Vicks," he whispered. "You're right, and most people here know it. And even if they don't, I do."

Smiling, she let him get back to his industry talk while she reveled in the way he made her feel. As out of her element as she felt during the meal, his touch let her know they were still together. And with the way he'd kept inching her skirt higher and higher, she had no doubt he'd show her just how close together they could get once they were back at his place.

For now, though, they were done, and without any additional attitude from Reed. The cast was still chatting as everyone stood, but people were polite enough to include her in their good-byes, so she didn't feel totally left out.

As she was headed toward the coat check with Dante, Saul called out, "Dante, one more thing before we leave."

Smiling at him, Vicky said, "I'll get my wrap. Go. Work."

He squeezed her fingers. "You're the best. Be right back."

Around the corner, she handed over the claim tags and waited.

"So, it's Vicky Stone. Why didn't you tell me who you were at Saul's party?"

Vicky's shoulders went tight under the black lace. Reed. Damn it. So much for a clean getaway. She plastered on a smile and turned to him as she took her silk shawl and wrapped it around her body. "It didn't really seem important."

"Of course it's important. Everything about a woman I plan to have in my bed is important." Reed reached out a hand and brushed a thumb over her cheek.

Ew. Vicky took a step back, putting a nice layer of distance between them. "I appreciate the offer, but I value my job. It would have been a really bad idea. Besides, I heard a rumor Saul caught some people in the house after the party and wasn't very happy about it." True enough, even if Jade's rumor mill wasn't grinding right. After all, Saul *had* caught her sneaking out.

"He might not have caught anyone if the other ladies hadn't been waiting for you to join us."

Double ew. He was exactly the kind of disgusting creep both Dante and Jade had said. Dinner threatened to come back up for a second showing—all over his designer suit.

• • •

"So, you don't think that'll be a problem?" Saul asked.

"Not at all," Dante said. Saul was way too stressed about a movie they hadn't even started filming yet. "If there's nothing else…?"

"No. Go. Have a great night. I'll see you tomorrow."

Thank goodness. He was about to turn toward the coat check when he heard Reed's voice. "He might not have caught anyone if the other ladies hadn't been waiting for you to join us."

Dante flashed back to the party, to the three women Reed had had in his room, to Vicky half naked and planning to crawl in bed with the asshole. Something inside him that he hadn't felt since the night the knife had gone into the muscle of his shoulder roared to life. He was done playing nice with this piece of shit. Rounding the corner, Dante grabbed Reed and yanked him away from Vicky. "You stay the fuck away from her, Russell. She's with me."

"Or you'll what? Go all Inferno on me?" Reed held up

his hands, mock-shaking them as if trying to ward Dante off. "Look at me, I'm terrified. You can't touch me, Palladino."

Fury boiled up inside him, and he was ready to threaten his own career by knocking Reed's head through a wall when Vicky said, "Back off, Dante."

"What?"

"I don't need a hero. It's under control."

Was she kidding? Reed had been moving toward her when Dante saw him. The guy was a predator. He knew it. *She* knew it. How the hell could she act like this was no big deal?

She laid a hand on his arm and met his eyes. "Please, Dante. Let's just go."

He was ready to do as she asked—they'd even turned around and headed toward the door—when Reed laughed. "Are you fucking kidding me?"

Every muscle in Dante's body tightened, ready to spring on his costar. "Go home, Russell."

"Just tell me I'm wrong. Tell me you aren't boning the waitress."

Dante spun on his heel and backed Russell against the wall outside the coat check. "You little piece of shit. You don't talk about her like that."

"My God, you *are*. Saul's going to love this."

Vicky was tugging at his arm, but Dante didn't care. He wasn't leaving until the jerk got a piece of his mind, and preferably a piece of his fist to go with it. "She's my best friend's sister, and Saul knows perfectly well why she's here. You're the one who likes to make trouble. What was the one chick? Seventeen? Sixteen?"

"Doesn't matter. Saul kicked her out."

"You filthy son of a bitch."

Vicky ducked under Dante's arm to stand between them. "Stop it. Let's just go. He isn't worth this."

"Fine." His fist flew past her face and slammed into the wall less than an inch from Reed's ear. "But you stay the hell away from Vicky if you know what's good for you."

It didn't quite register why, but Vicky's face went tight as he said the words, her eyes narrowed in what looked like anger. Lips pressed in a hard line, she shoved him toward the door.

Reed, on the other hand, seemed to find the whole thing funny. Another laugh burst from his lips. "At least my jailbait was only looking to bang one actor. Seems your little whore will take whichever movie star dick comes along."

Before Dante could move, Vicky twisted around and smacked Reed. "You know, I used to believe tabloids had to exaggerate to sell papers. Then I met you. There isn't a level of hell deep enough for you to burn in, you disgusting piece of shit."

She was out the door a second later, Dante trailing behind her. "I told you. I *warned you* about the type of person he was, Vicky. If you'd only listened—"

They hadn't even reached his car when she spun on him, her hands flat on his chest as she shoved. "Screw you, Dante. I *told you* that I didn't need a fucking hero. I had everything under control until you decided to storm in, guns blazing, and blow everything out of proportion. Yes, he's an ass—a colossal ass—but I was dealing with him fine without you deciding blows needed to be exchanged. Without you making it obvious to him and anyone in hearing distance that not only am I sleeping with you, but I was stupid enough to think about fucking him, too. God!"

The heat leaked out of him. She didn't understand. She still didn't see how awful Reed was. "Vicky, he never would have let you walk out of there."

"Then I would have asked for help. But there was a whole world of possibilities of how that could have gone down that didn't involve him publicly calling me a whore, you punching a damn wall, or me slapping him—all in front of your boss and your costars. Damn it." She raked her hands through her hair, yanking on the golden strands in frustration. "I'm starting to think you really were looking for a way out of whatever we have going on, because you sure as hell ruined any chance of the people you work with taking me seriously."

"Don't you throw me under that bus. If you hadn't planned to fuck Reed in the first place, we wouldn't be having this conversation."

"We wouldn't be having a conversation at all because I wouldn't have talked to you that night, either."

"Maybe that would have been better!" he snapped.

She stepped back as if he'd slapped her. Dante shook his head, reaching a hand toward her. "I'm sorry, Vicks, I didn't mean it."

"No. You're right. Maybe that would have been better." She backed away from him—one step after another, the gulf between them widening until it seemed uncrossable. "I'll take a cab. I think it's best if I sleep at my apartment tonight."

Then she was gone, disappearing into the nighttime crowd like a phantom.

Somehow he'd gone from hero to zero in the space of five minutes, and he had no idea how to come back from it.

Chapter Sixteen

Vicky slept like crap. The tossing and turning would have been bad enough, but the only breaks had been via dreams of all the ways things could have gone worse. If she *had* gone to Reed's room that night and wound up taking part in his little orgy just to earn her post-divorce sex badge from Jade, she would have lost her job and possibly worse.

And if she'd shown up and said no? She spent the rest of her night thinking of all the horrible, violent ways that might have ended.

She woke up in the morning tired, cranky, and feeling tormented. Dante had probably already imagined all those things and worse. His reaction to Reed cornering her might not have been necessary, but in hindsight, she did understand it. But when she left, he hadn't tried to stop her. He hadn't followed her when she'd gone to get a cab. He hadn't even called or texted to make sure she got home okay, so now she didn't know what to do.

And she'd left the damn party binder at his place. Luckily she had digital copies of everything on her laptop, but she couldn't help but wonder if she'd left it on purpose—knowing in her heart something like this would happen. Leaving it so she had a reason to go back.

Who was she kidding? She didn't need to wonder. Of course she had.

The fight was stupid. *That* was the reason she hadn't slept. She felt guilty for lashing out at him like she had, and her dreams had just been reminders of all the reasons she'd been in the wrong. She was already on her way to Brentwood to talk to him when she realized he wasn't home. The cast had a read-through today or something. He'd be at the studio, likely with his phone turned off.

She couldn't apologize, but at least she could get some work done on the party, make sure staff was lined up and everything. She pulled off the next exit and headed toward Elegant Entertainment. If nothing else, at least she hadn't screwed this up. Even with her weird hours, she'd managed to come in under budget, and she knew the party would be a hit with Dante, Evan, and their guests. She couldn't wait to see Mathew's face.

The door had barely closed behind her when Mathew's secretary said, "Oh, I guess I don't need to call you." She hung up the phone. "Mr. Collins wanted to see you in his office as soon as you arrived."

Weird. She hadn't been in the office in weeks. Why did he need her now? Had someone found out she was doing the party and bitched about it? Did he need to know exactly when she was resuming her normal schedule as a waitress? Or had the fight been a bigger deal than she thought, and

Dante had called to cancel?

She almost laughed at the last. He wouldn't have done that. That was blackmail-Dante not race-to-the-rescue-Dante. She was still giggling at the thought when she pushed open Mathew's door. "You wanted to see me?"

He tipped his head up, his face tight enough that he looked like he'd just Botoxed everything the night before.

"I did, and you can wipe that smile off your face. I don't know what the hell you thought you were pulling, but it ends now. Clear out your stuff immediately."

"What?"

"I know all about your *extracurricular activities*, and quite frankly, I'm embarrassed for you. I had this crazy idea in my head when I hired you that, as the sister of a movie star, you understood the Hollywood game better than most of the women who work here, but obviously I was wrong. If you want to sleep your way to the top, you can do it on your own time."

Vicky couldn't move. She couldn't breathe. Dante hadn't called to cancel the party. He'd called to make good on his threat, only now he didn't just have her slipup at Saul's to hold over her head—he had all their dates, all their nights together. He could even provide a paper trail with their visit to his doctor. How could she have been so stupid? "Mathew, let me explain…"

"There's nothing you can say, Vicky. You're fired. Get the hell out of my building. Your last check will be in the mail, *assuming* Palladino doesn't call off the entire thing." When she didn't move fast enough, Mathew straightened his tie, focusing on it instead of her, and said, "If you do not walk out of here voluntarily and quietly in the next thirty seconds, I will call security to throw you out."

Vicky's lip quivered, her entire body following suit. She trembled the entire way to his office door. Outside, she sagged against the wall, barely able to breathe.

He'd done it. He'd said he would, and he had. Dante had gotten her fired. With no income, possibly not even a last check for all the work she'd been doing, she'd be lucky to cover next month's rent without having to ask for help. All this time trying to make it on her own, to create a solid future, and one stupid decision to let herself fall for Dante Palladino was forcing her to be the one thing she'd promised herself she'd never be again. He'd turned her into a damsel in distress.

It was all she could do to hold the tears in until she made it back to her Acura with the box of personal items from her locker. She'd thought she'd been building something new, something better, but now she had nothing left, not even the walls around her heart. She leaned against the steering wheel and sobbed.

How could she have been so stupid? She'd warned herself time and again that she shouldn't get involved with Dante, or anyone. And in regard to him specifically, even her brother had warned her away. Bad news was bad news, no matter how much time had passed.

She'd done this all to herself. There wasn't even anyone else she could blame. Dante had *told* her he would report her to her boss. It was the only reason she'd gone out with him in the first place. She'd *known*, and still she kept questioning the dichotomy of the guy who'd blackmailed her and the one who seemed so *sweet*. She should have been smarter than to trust a devil in angel's clothing.

And now she had nothing. No guy. No job. And soon enough, she'd lose her apartment.

There was nothing left. If she couldn't find a job in the next week, she'd have no choice but to call Evan and beg for help. Or Jade. Or Mom. Or someone.

She'd thought she'd hit rock bottom when Brandon had left. But that was nothing compared to this. At least she'd crawled away from the divorce with her car and enough to pay it off, put down first and last on the apartment, and buy some clothes to interview in.

There was no crawling away from Dante with anything, because even the job he'd promised her…she knew in her heart he'd cancel the party or let Mathew hand it over to someone else. She'd be lucky if he didn't claim her hours were a lie. No. Dante Palladino had taken everything from her, and she didn't even have the self-respect left to try to claw her way out of the emotional gutter where he'd left her.

• • •

Dante was done. The read-through had taken far longer than he'd hoped, and the whole time he'd been thinking of nothing except getting to Vicky and apologizing. She was right. He'd overstepped with Reed and made them both look bad in the process. For years, he'd thought he had control over his anger, but the only thing it took was seeing someone he cared about in a dangerous position and all of it came right back out again.

As soon as they were dismissed, he raced to his car. There was no way he was risking another minute spent at the studio answering a question that could be as easily dealt with through text or email. Vicky needed to be in person, and she needed to be now.

He tried calling on the way to her apartment, but she never answered. In fact, with how quickly the calls went to voicemail, he was pretty sure she was rejecting them immediately. He didn't leave a message. Nothing he could say over the phone would come out right. One slip and it'd be all over with no chance of recovery.

The block around her complex was filled with cars at this time of day. He didn't know why, and he didn't care. There was one spot. It said no parking, but the window on that closed in fifteen minutes. Surely there wouldn't be a cop around *waiting* to ticket someone. He pulled in and threw the car into park. If she wasn't home, he'd be back in under a minute. If she was, he'd just have to take his chances. It'd be worth the ticket as long as he had her back.

Racing up the stairs to her door, Dante almost tripped as her neighbor stepped outside. The man had probably been about five-nine, but now with the way he stooped, leaning on his cane, he looked more like five-six. "I wouldn't knock on that door if I were you."

"Which door would that be?" Dante asked, a little amused, but mostly worried.

"Vicky's. We all saw you here with her a couple weeks back. Then she's gone like she doesn't even live here, and when she does finally show up it's all slamming doors and cursing. Seems like someone sprayed water at a wildcat, and I'm betting that someone's you." The man hobbled toward the stairs.

"How do you know she's mad at me?"

He chuckled. "I looked you up on that internet thing my

grandkids like so much. They used to call you the Inferno."

"That's right."

"Well, Vicky's been hollering about burning someplace down and wondering how the Inferno'd like that. So…call it a lucky guess." He took the stairs one laborious tread at a time. "Knock at your own risk."

Dante waited until the old man was gone. There was no way she was *that* pissed over last night. Still, his knock was tentative.

The door flew open, and Vicky stood there, her hair wild and her red face streaked with sweat and tears. Her hands clenched and unclenched as if she couldn't decide whether to punch him, slap him, or something else entirely. "What the hell do you want? Haven't you done enough?"

He'd never seen her this mad, never even heard Evan talk about her like this. "Vicks, I came to apologize."

"Apologize? You think you can just walk up to my door, say sorry, and suddenly everything's going to be all right again?" She stepped onto the landing, her rage and hurt making the air around her a physical thing that pushed him away until his back was pressed to the railing. "You. Got. Me. Fired! I have *nothing* left, Dante, and certainly nothing left for you. There isn't a damn thing you can say that will make my world okay again."

"Vicky, I didn't…" He didn't even know how to finish the sentence. Someone must have overheard the fight with Reed last night and word got back to her boss.

"You didn't what? Didn't *mean to*? Didn't *think*? Didn't figure it mattered because you could swoop in and save me again?"

Shit. She thought he'd *actually* gone to her boss? "I

didn't get you fired, not intentionally, at least. If someone overheard yesterday and—"

"You know what? It doesn't even matter if you made the call or just precipitated it. We'd been so fucking careful because you *knew* what the rules were. You *knew* we were breaking them." She shoved at his pecs, the force of her hands doing little, but the force of her pain crushing him. Tears lit her eyes, and he knew it was all she could do not to hit him like she had Reed. "I told you. I didn't want a fucking hero. I didn't need one. But like everyone else in my life, you thought I was weak. You thought you could be the guy to fix everything, even if you were the one who destroyed it. Well, guess what, Dante? You broke everything. You broke me, and I sure as hell don't want you to stick around to try to pick up the pieces."

She turned around, strode back into her apartment, and slammed the door, leaving him there to listen as she burst into sobs inside—farther away from him than the few feet of actual distance.

Now he wished she had slapped him. Physical violence he understood. He would have let her hit him until she collapsed, and then he would have held her until she stopped crying. They could have worked back from that. This? He didn't have a clue what to do with this.

Especially since she was right. His thoughts proved it. He wanted to shelter her in his arms and make her world right again. He wanted to be her hero. He wanted to save the day.

Instead, he'd taken away everything that she'd managed to build back into her life after her divorce.

He wasn't the hero.

For the first time in his life, he realized he was the villain.

Chapter Seventeen

The call from Elegant Entertainment came first thing the next day. "In case you haven't heard the news, Mr. Palladino, I regret to inform you that we had to let Vicky Stone go."

The little troll made it sound like he was actually upset. Dante wanted to reach through the phone and throttle him. "Can I ask what exactly prompted this decision?"

"I'm sorry, but we can't discuss matters like that with clients."

"That's not so much of a problem since I'm no longer a client."

"Mr. Palladino, I assure you, we have any number of planners who can finish—"

Dante squeezed his cell phone so hard he was surprised the thing didn't crack. "I remember telling you, very explicitly, that Vicky Stone, and only Vicky Stone, was to handle this party. I expect every dime I've paid you for anything beyond her time to be returned to me immediately, or I'll be in contact with my lawyers regarding your breach of contract."

"But...but... The planning is finished. All that was left was assigning staff for the event and overseeing them. Any of my people can do that."

"Any of them could, but I specifically hired Vicky to. You fired her. Either hire her back or the party is off, at least as far as you're concerned." Dante pulled onto Venice.

"I will not be bullied, Mr. Palladino."

"Good. That's a great personality trait to have. I expect a full refund by close of business today." He thumbed the phone off and raked a hand through his hair. What he was going to do about the party, he didn't know, but he sure as hell wasn't rewarding that little troll for firing Vicky.

Juan was sitting on his front stoop when Dante pulled into the driveway. He jogged up to the car, climbed in, and said, "Drive."

Nothing was said until they were out of the neighborhood. "So, did you make a decision?"

"Yes and no." Juan looked out the window at the passing scenery, probably not taking in any of it. "The recruiter did some legwork for me. He passed Mom's résumé around and found her a job — a good one. It will be better for my mom and brother out there. Cheaper housing, safer neighborhood — it's everything we don't have here."

"That's great. What's the problem?"

"Graduation. They're already after Tico." He didn't have to ask who *they* were, because it sure as hell wasn't the college. "If I wait it out until graduation in the spring... I don't know, man. Tico's going to figure all this out, and if he tells them, it could go bad."

Dante scrubbed his face. This should have been simple.

Juan had a chance at a real future, but it was like Lee Cor-bitt all over again. He didn't want to think about the kind of damage that could happen if the local boys caught wind of Juan leaving and taking their newest recruit with him. "What do you want to do?"

"I want you to tell me I'm not crazy." He pulled a sheet of paper out of his pocket. "I'm going to be done with all my graduation requirements in January except one. I talked to my guidance counselor. She said I could finish the class online and still graduate. I wouldn't get to walk across the stage, but I could get my family out of here in January. Is it stupid? Do you think I can keep it from Tico long enough? Or should I just stay here? I mean, this is the only home we've ever had."

"I think…" Damn. There were a million thoughts going through his head. "I think if you pass up this opportunity, you're going to regret it. I think maybe you could move your mom and Tico out as soon as you can. Whoever hired your mom probably won't be ready to move them for another month or two, but every day they're here is a risk of retalia-tion against you and your family. She'll have time to quietly get Tico enrolled in a middle school out there, but not so much time that you can't keep it a secret. Once they're gone, you can stay at my place while you finish up the semester. It's a hell of a haul to school, but it wouldn't be for long, and your family would be safe. Then we move you out east as soon as the semester is over."

"I can't ask you to do that."

"You don't have to ask, I offered." But he hadn't de-manded or pushed like he had with Vicky. "All you have to do is say yes."

Juan slapped him on the arm. "Hells yeah, man! This'll be such a load off Mom's mind. I can't ever repay you for this, you know."

"Make the most of the chance. That's payment enough." He circled back to the little house and dropped Juan off. As he drove away, he couldn't help but wonder why it was so easy to *offer* help to Juan, but when it came to Vicky, he'd jumped in every time, even when she'd told him not to.

. . .

"What do you mean you won't be at the party? It's my birthday, Vicky. I'm leaving my *pregnant wife* home so I can come to this thing you planned for me and Dante." Evan sounded pissed, actually beyond pissed.

"For starters, I don't work for the company anymore, so it isn't my account. Second, I'm not speaking to Dante." *Because he got me fired just so he could play hero and try to swoop in and fix things after.* Even thinking it made her sick. "And third...we'll do dinner or something before you leave."

She could almost hear him silently ranting on the other end of the line. It involved half sighs, exasperated grunting, and a few other noises she couldn't identify. "Damn it. Stasia's going to kill me—you were the whole reason she said yes to this. What the hell happened with you and Dante anyway? You said you met at that party, and the next thing you were getting a promotion—"

She packed another box of books. If she was lucky, she'd be able to find a new job, but she wanted to be prepared if she had to move out in a hurry. "It wasn't a promotion, it was a temporary thing. This party only. It's...complicated."

She had to come clean. He was her brother, and she'd spill eventually anyway. "Dante and I started seeing each other, and that fucked everything up. I should have listened to you way back when you told me he was bad news. If I'd avoided him for life like you suggested, at least I'd still have my low-man-on-the-totem-pole job."

"Uh…"

A book in hand and halfway in the box, Vicky paused. "What do you mean by *uh*?"

"You know I only said that shit to keep the two of you apart because you were about to get married, right?"

Well, logically that made sense—all of it but the *only* part. "Because he's a troublemaker and was going to try to get me to screw him or something and fuck up my wedding."

"More like because it was obvious you two were rapidly developing a thing for each other and *that* was going to fuck up your wedding."

Vicky swallowed hard. "You mean there was no horrible past that I was avoiding?"

"No. I mean, I'm sure he has a past, but not what I let you believe. In my defense, I had no clue Brandon was going to turn out to be such a jackass."

The book fell from numb fingers to land in the box. "So what you're saying is Dante isn't a jackass?"

"Not at all. Like I said, if I'd known, I would have pushed the two of you together rather than shoving you apart. He's a good guy—one of the best I know, actually."

The kind to blackmail her to keep her out of harm's way, like Jade suggested. The kind to orchestrate a sudden party so she could prove herself at work. The kind who had a "little brother" along with a charity to keep kids off the street.

Vicky leaned against the wall, her head banging it quietly. "So, you're saying he's not the type who'd have gone out of his way to get me fired."

"What? Hell, no. If anything, he'd do just what you said and try to help you get a leg up at Elegant." *Which he totally had* earlier. It was just this latest stupidity that had thrown her off the deep end. "The whole hero thing might not exactly be in his DNA, but it's pretty fucking close." When she didn't respond, Evan said, "Vicky, what's going on?"

"I…I don't know, but I think I might have fucked up worse than you did with Stasia in Vegas." And Evan had done one hell of a job there.

"Damn it. I'll be there this weekend. We'll figure it out."

Unfortunately, she had a feeling this was a job too big for even her superhero brother to fix. She was so screwed.

• • •

"Is the damn party on or not?" Evan sounded so pissed there was no question he'd already spoken to Vicky.

Dante slumped down in his chair, staring at the party binder she'd left behind. "I don't know."

"Okay, then can you tell me what the hell you did to get my sister fired?"

If he sank any lower, he'd be on the floor. "I don't know. Actually, that's not true. I did something stupid, the wrong person overheard the wrong thing, and it must've gotten back to her boss."

"Fine. How are you going to fix it?"

Easier said than done; Vicky wanted nothing to do with him. "She won't let me fix anything."

"Dante, man, you are my best friend, but you're a moron sometimes. She doesn't want you to *rescue* her. That doesn't mean you can't fix whatever the hell happened."

Evan made it sound so easy, like he could just flip open the binder and find the answer to life, the universe, and everything. And he really doubted *Hitchhiker's Guide to the Galaxy* had it right with regard to it being the number forty-two. "Like you fixed things with Stasia? A song and a ring?"

"You're not this stupid. Stasia didn't forgive me because of the song or the ring. She forgave me because I stopped being a selfish little boy and figured out what I needed to do to be a man. To be *her* man."

"Unfortunately, I don't think Vicky will let me be her man again." Dante frowned as he realized Evan hadn't beaten him up about their relationship at all. "Speaking of, aren't you going to tell me to stay the hell away from your little sister?"

"Why would I do that? You two were kind of meant to be, or all this wouldn't have happened. You're both adults. What you do with this relationship, or any other, isn't exactly my business. What is…is the party. I have a pregnant wife willing to let me fly out for the day, but if there's no party, I'd rather stay home."

Dante knew he should just cancel. It made the most sense, especially since he'd fired Elegant Entertainment and had *nothing* ready or even organized. He was about to tell Evan to stay home when his phone buzzed with an incoming text. "Just a second."

He thumbed over to the text screen.

Hey Inferno,

YOU TOLD ME TO KEEP YOU UP-TO-DATE ON JINX. THINGS WITH THE FAMILY DIDN'T WORK OUT. SHE'S BACK AT THE SHELTER AND ON SHORT TIME. WHAT DO YOU WANT ME TO DO?

The dog. The mutt Vicky had fallen in love with at Pacific Park. He had no idea what to do with that information.

He had no idea what to do with anything.

Flipping back to the call, he dropped his hand, intending to slam it on the table. Instead, it thumped against the binder.

"So? On or off?"

Dante barely heard Evan's question; he was too busy flipping through the pages in front of him. It was all there. All of it, right fucking there.

"Party's on. I have a lot of calls to make, though, so I'll see you Saturday. Tell Stasia I said thanks, and give her belly a kiss for me." He hung up and flipped back to the other screen, typing as fast as his fingers could move over the tiny keys.

THAT DOG ISN'T DYING ON MY WATCH. I'M NOT SURE WHERE, BUT I'M GOING TO FIND HER A HOME PERSONALLY.

He didn't even wait for a response. He had a party to plan, numbers to crunch, checks to send, and if everything went right, a relationship to save.

• • •

Saturdays weren't usually for lunch with Jade, but Vicky was glad they'd made an exception this once. And Jade had gone all out, splurging to take her to the Polo Lounge in Beverly Hills.

Evan's flight had gotten in late, and she hadn't wanted

to keep him from the party. This was her mess. She'd either figure out a way to fix it or she wouldn't. Running to her brother for help after getting mad at Dante for storming to her rescue seemed bassackward, anyway.

Leave it to Jade to suggest lunch and drinks as an alternative to brotherly love.

"What do you want to do now? The party's still on for a few hours. I don't think leaving you alone is a good idea." Jade slid a pair of sunglasses onto her nose as they stepped outside.

"I don't know. I'd suggest shopping, but with no money…"

"Oh, no, did someone get fired?" The voice came from right behind her, so familiar and so close she had to fight the urge to overreact. Instead she turned slowly to face a grinning Reed, who said, "I heard you got in trouble for fucking some guy at an industry party a few weeks back. Really bad form, especially for the sister of an A-lister. Better hope this doesn't damage your brother's reputation. Oh, that's right, he and his wife are already porn stars, aren't they?"

She heard all the crap about Evan, but her brain had stuttered over the party comment. "It was you."

"No, but it could have been."

"I mean, you're the one who reported me to Mathew. You said I fucked Dante at that party. Or that I fucked you. It really doesn't matter who you said I did it with."

"Funny thing is, your boss didn't seem to care. It was like he knew you were a whore all along." Reed shrugged, grin turning into a cocky smirk that Vicky wished she could wipe right off his face, but she was stunned silent.

"Hey, is this your car?" Jade called from the street, running her hand lovingly over the hood of a red sports car.

As if he hadn't realized they were together, Reed turned on the charm. "It is. I'm just wondering where the valet went."

She waved a hand dismissively. "He's grabbing my baby. Ferrari 458, right?"

"Italia."

The whistle that came from between Jade's full lips was low and sexy. "I bet it set you back a pretty penny."

"That it did." He started to walk toward her, but just then the valet drove up in Jade's black convertible.

She grabbed Vicky's hand, pulling her toward the waiting car, and yelled over her shoulder, "Good choice in color, too. Douche bag red suits you."

It wasn't until she'd climbed into the passenger seat that Vicky caught sight of the side of Reed's Ferrari. There was a scratch from tail to driver's door, metal gleaming through the bright red paint. She could barely suppress a smile as the valet called Reed over, and Jade pulled into traffic.

"Sorry about that little charade, but no one gets to call my best girl a whore and get away with it."

"I love you."

Jade pulled into an open parking spot and idled there. "Then I think it's time you let me give you some tough love."

This wasn't going to be good. "Jade…"

She waved a perfectly manicured hand. "You just found out that it wasn't Dante or even your fight that got you fired. It was that arrogant fucktard we left behind us at the hotel. Sure, Dante overstepped, but he also did his best to help you out of a tight spot *without* overstepping before that."

"I know."

"And, quite frankly, I've never seen you as happy as

when you were with him. Even that first day at Mortensen's place when you said all you wanted was your work ID back...you *glowed* after that fucking kiss."

"But this wasn't supposed to happen. My deal with you was just that I'd have sex. That was all. I screwed up my life by getting involved." Vicky let out a deep sigh. "I'm going to end up screwing up his if I get reinvolved now. I need to fix me, just like I did before."

"Uh...that's not really true." Jade bit her lip. "You see, I kind of knew this would happen."

"What?"

Jade shrugged. "You don't *need* a man, Vicky. You never did, but you've always done better, *been happier*, when you had a partner in crime. If I wasn't gone so much, maybe you'd have been perfectly happy if it was me, but you need that energy of someone in your life who always has your back, even when you don't need them there."

"But isn't that leaning on someone like I always did? I don't want to be taken care of anymore."

"So, don't let him take care of you. You can build you while you build a relationship, and from what I've seen, he's a good guy to have in your corner, even if all he does is stand there and stare down any assfaces that come close." Jade reached over and rested her hand on Vicky's. "Face facts, Vicky, you don't do casual sex. It never would have worked for you. I figured the deal would either help you realize that or wind up with you in the arms of a great guy. It's up to you to decide which one of those things happened with Dante."

Jade was right. Everything she'd said had been spot-on. The big question was could Vicky resist the lure of falling into the damsel-in-distress trap? Could she be strong enough to stand on her own? She wanted to try. Damn, she wanted to try. "There's only one way for me to be sure."

"Does this mean we get to storm the castle?"

Vicky couldn't help but laugh. "You're my hero."

"Nope, I'm your bitch. Heroes save the day. Bitches key the cars. Get your job descriptions right."

"I love you."

"You said that already."

"Fine. I'll do you one better." Vicky scrunched up her nose as she thought of all the things she could say that Jade would dismiss out of hand. Then she said, "You know, if we were lesbians, I'd totally want to do you."

"I know."

"You know I've often wondered if you were a lesbian, or at least bisexual."

"If I had a quarter for every time someone—"

Laughing, Vicky pressed a hand over Jade's lips. "Okay, you win! I don't want to know. But thank you."

"You're welcome. Now let's get your bony ass to the party." Jade winked, threw her convertible into gear, and pulled into traffic, weaving between cars as if her life depended on it.

Vicky kind of hoped her future did.

Chapter Eighteen

"So, how did you pull this off if you canceled the contract with Elegant Entertainment?" Evan had a drink in his hand and leaned against the railing of the deck.

Dante stared out at the yard filled with tents and decorations. Vicky had done awesome work, pulling together elements of Evan's characters and his to create something that spoke to both their careers without being tacky about it—subtle enough they spoke to the men themselves as well. Navy blue and deep crimson decorated off-white tents with gold and silver accents, pulling everything together into a grown-up superhero party.

He had to turn away. Looking at it made him think of her.

Instead, he reached down and scratched the head of the dog sitting by his side. Because that didn't make him think of her at all. Right.

He tried not to sigh. "She left all her notes. I called

the vendors, explained the situation, and said I'd pay them exactly what Elegant would have to just do what they were going to do anyway. They all jumped at not losing the sales at the last minute."

"And what about you? Did you talk to her yet?" Evan sipped his beer like he hadn't a care in the world. It was the first time he'd even mentioned Vicky. Dante wasn't sure whether to thank him or beg for information—if Evan had any.

"I haven't figured out what to say. I mean, the plan is after everyone leaves, I'm going to go over, but..."

Evan shrugged and waved at someone out by one of the tents. "Why didn't you just ask her to come? Maybe she would have."

"If she wanted to be here at all, she would be. I mean, *you're* here. She hasn't seen you in months." Dante threw back his beer. "Besides, you ask that like you think she'd enjoy making a scene at our birthday party."

"And you say that like you know it would be a scene."

Too true. It wasn't that he was afraid to talk to Vicky. He was afraid of all the ways she could potentially tell him to fuck off for good. "I just don't want her to feel like she can't say whatever she needs to say. The only chance we have is if we put everything on the table."

Evan clapped him on the shoulder. "It'll all work out. If it helps anything, I regret keeping you guys apart five years ago."

"She was getting married." Dante shrugged, his shoulders feeling far too heavy.

"She was getting married to an asshole who was going to break her heart. I should have seen it. If nothing else, I should have seen how much happier she was around you than she was around him." Evan drained the last of his beer. "I'm really sorry I wasn't a better friend. Or a better brother."

"If you think either of us blame you, you're wrong. I never would have met Vicky if not for you." He couldn't blame Evan for keeping them apart, not when he'd screwed up so many different ways since finally reuniting with her. He just wanted the damn party over so he could figure out how to tell her he had her back, whatever she wanted to do. He'd stand by as support, but he wasn't going to jump in anymore unless she wanted him to. He'd say…

"Earth to birthday boy." Evan's voice shook him from his musings. "You probably should have talked to her *pre*-party. You're not even here, man."

"Sorry. I called a couple times, but I hung up before the phone even rang. It would have been better that way, but I was an idiot. So now I'm here, when I should be there."

"And I'm here when I should be home. But you're my best friend, and she's my sister. Stasia told me not to come back until this shit is fixed."

"You have a baby on the way."

"I know."

"Your wife is a hard-ass."

Evan laughed, the sound shattering the tension on the deck. "I know that, too. In the meantime…beer?"

"Yeah." Not that it would change anything, but at least he'd have something to hold on to besides the dog's stupid leash. Without warning, Jinx's ears perked up, flopping forward, showing off her dalmatian side. Before he could say a word, she launched from her spot on the deck, tearing the leash right out of his grip. "Damn it!"

Dante raced after her. He'd had the dog less than a week—the last thing he wanted was for her to get overprotective and bite one of his guests.

Or lick one to death. Jinx stood at the front door, a body under her. Said body couldn't stop giggling as she tried to push the dog's face away. For the first time, Dante was really glad about Jinx's single-minded nature. It gave him a chance to catch his breath and get his head on straight before Vicky sat up and ran a hand through her golden-blond hair. "I finally show up to your party only to discover you gave yourself the one thing I always wanted. What the hell is a girl supposed to think about that?"

. . .

It had only been a week, so why did looking at him now feel like she hadn't seen him in forever? Then he just stood there. Vicky would have thought time had frozen if not for the metronome quality of Jinx's wagging tail. Where the hell had the dog even come from? Had Dante invited its new owners? That seemed ridiculously unlikely, but he wasn't answering her.

"Dante?"

He shook off whatever he was thinking, strode over, and held out a hand. "I really wasn't expecting you."

Oh, God. Did he have someone else here as his date? She couldn't imagine he'd pull that, what with Evan being here. "I can...come back later."

"No." He grabbed her fingers and helped her to stand, taking Jinx's leash. "I want you here. I just didn't think you'd come."

No other woman. She *really* needed to stop thinking all the bad things about him that came to her mind. He wasn't Brandon. He sure as hell wasn't Reed. Dante had never been anything but good to her. "I almost didn't. Then I ran into Reed, and he made me realize just what a jerk I'd been."

"No. I was the… Reed? What the hell? If that little shit is causing problems again, I swear I'm going to…" His face purpled for a moment, and then it was as if all the anger leaked out of him. "I swear I'm going to let you fight your own battles unless you ask for backup."

"Well, that's the other thing I realized after the Reed Russell run-in. I'm only afraid of letting people help me when they're really close. And by really close I mean live-in close. My mother, Evan, Brandon…you. When Jade keyed Reed's car, I wanted to high-five her. It never even occurred to me to be angry."

"She keyed his car?"

Vicky couldn't help but smile at the expression on Dante's face. His eyes practically gleamed with joy. "And then she called the color douche bag red. I'm pretty sure he'll be selling that Ferrari below market value very soon."

"I'd tell all my friends, but none of them need a douche-mobile." Dante reached a hand toward her slowly, as if he thought she'd bolt. She leaned into his touch instead. "I'm sorry I tried to take over your life."

"You didn't."

"Yeah. I kind of did. I changed your job. I had you basically move in with me. Upended your schedule. I changed everything, and I tried to control everything." His thumb traced her cheekbone. "I wanted so badly to help make your life better that I forgot to let it be your life." He let his hand fall, stepped over to the console table near the door, and picked up an envelope.

Then, in a rush of air, Evan was there. "I need a car, and I need a plane ticket booked. Now, you two!"

Dante was digging for keys, and Vicky took in her brother's panicked eyes. "What's wrong? What happened?"

"My wife's in labor, and I'm here listening to you guys debate your future. I'm going to go become a father. And my first bit of fatherly guidance is going to be to tell the two of you to work your shit out. Because if you're still fighting when I show up at the hospital, it's not going to be pretty." He snatched the keys out of Dante's hand and was out the door.

Vicky yelled after him. "Congratulations! And give Stasia my love!" She winced as she turned back around. "We did that, didn't we?"

"Another thing that was my fault. I wanted you to be in my life so badly I concocted this party when I knew Stasia was due soon." He picked the envelope back up and held it out to her. "Speaking of the party, this is for you. And before you say anything, it's not a gift and it's not a handout."

Vicky eyed the thing warily as she took it. "What is it then?"

"After I canceled the contract with Elegant, I used your binder to make sure the party still happened. I took the final figure that I would have paid to your asshole boss, subtracted all the costs, and the rest is in there. For you."

Shaking her head, Vicky tried to hand the check back to him. "I got paid for my time working on the party, Dante. You don't owe me this."

"You want me to give it to Mathew Collins?" He reached for the check. "Because I can do that. I just preferred the idea of giving it to the person who did all the work."

Not a handout. Maybe a bit of a hand up, but she knew Mathew made a lot more than his employees ever saw. "No. I'll take it. It'll keep me in groceries and an apartment for a while longer."

Hurt clouded his eyes. "I'd kind of hoped that you and I were bridging the gap we opened up." He tipped his head toward Jinx. "I mean, she likes me okay, but the running tackle kind of proves she wants you around."

"You mean she *is* yours?"

"I was thinking more along the lines of she's *ours*. Unless I broke our relationship beyond repair."

The dog rubbed her head against Vicky's leg, tail moving a mile a minute. Dante was offering her the kind of home she'd always wanted. Security, love…a dog. She shook her head. "I'm not moving in. Not yet. We need to make sure we're okay, and I need to find another job. I'm not going to be a kept woman again. I refuse."

"Does that mean we're breaking up?"

"Hell, no. It means you're going to spend every day wooing me back. I don't care how many hours you're on set, if I'm pounding the pavement looking for work, I expect a foot massage before bed every night."

"I thought you weren't going to live here."

She wrinkled her nose at him and his logic. "And then I'll scratch Jinx on the head and drive home."

"Every night?"

"Every night."

Dante shrugged but couldn't hide his smile. "That's

going to get old."

"It sure is, so you better woo me back fast."

Dropping the leash, Dante swept her into his arms instead. "How's this for a first step: I don't want to just be your life partner. I want to be your business partner. No…investor. There are at least ten people here who wanted the name of my party planner. If you're willing to take a small loan from me—we can get you set up."

Vicky caught her lip in her teeth. Her own business? But this *was* a handout. "It sounds great, but I don't want your money. That kind of rescuing is what messed us up the first time."

"I'm not giving you the money, Vicks. I'm offering you a loan. I'll charge interest if you want. But if you pull off half a dozen parties like this, you'll be able to pay me back and then some. I'm not giving you your future, I'm just trying to remove the roadblocks in your way so you can earn it. And before you ask why…you know why. I love you, and I want to see you succeed at this. Will you do that for me? Will you let me be there to watch you shove your new company in Mathew Collins's face?"

Now that would be a dream come true.

Who was she kidding? Her dream was standing right in front of her and had been all along. Only this time she was awake, and she finally realized she got to keep him.

"I love you, too, you crazy man. Let's do it. Let's take on the damn world."

"Together?"

"Definitely."

Epilogue

Dante had cursed the traffic for the last hour. He was so fucking late it wasn't even funny. First filming had run over by days. Then his flight to the States was delayed. And now Los Angeles traffic. He couldn't cut a break.

And he'd promised Vicky he'd be back for this.

Finally he managed to find a parking space and then raced to her brand-new office. In only the few months he'd spent on location, she'd built her business enough to pay him back and get a bank loan in her own name to rent the space. Hiring a secretary was next on her list.

But tonight was the ribbon cutting.

He opened the door just in time to see her take a pair of giant scissors to the gold ribbon wrapped around the company logo. It fell open to reveal a red-and-gold fire. He'd argued against the name—loudly. But she'd insisted that since he'd been the one to help her get her start, she was naming the place after him. Besides, she'd argued, that was how other people had found her in the first place.

Thus, Inferno Party and Entertainment was born.

Vicky spoke to the friends and family and clients gathered, owning the space.

He might have promised he'd be here, but this was her show, and he sure as hell wasn't going to steal her spotlight. She'd dressed to match the logo, her halter shifting from black at the bottom through shades of red right up to the gold wrap around her shoulders. Just as she finished her speech, she caught sight of him near the door and broke into a grin. "Once again, thank you all for coming. You have no idea how much this company means to me. Enjoy your food and champagne."

She didn't rush across the space. He could tell she wanted to by the way she kept jerking to a stop every time someone caught her attention with a question or a compliment or whatever they were saying. If he didn't intercede, he'd never get his welcome-home kiss.

Dante strode through the crowd, people naturally moving aside as he walked, making way for his bulk. "Excuse me, mind if I steal the CEO? I have a party I need to discuss with her."

"You can steal me anytime." Vicky grinned up at him, then nodded at her guests. "I'll be right back."

"Take your time," the woman said. "I know I would."

Any thought their interlude might be secret was dashed, but he didn't care. He wanted to kiss his girlfriend properly, and he didn't feel like having a damn audience. She pulled him through the door at the back of the space and into her actual office — the other room serving as entrance and meeting area.

"I thought you'd *never* get here." Vicky wrapped her arms around his neck and stood on tiptoe to press her lips to his.

"Believe me, I debated skydiving as a quicker means of arrival, but I was afraid I'd miss my mark."

Her hand cupped him between his legs. "Oh, I don't know. I think if we give it a try, you'll hit your mark."

Dante's eyes rolled back in his head. He wanted her more than he wanted to breathe, but he'd convinced himself he could wait. "Your party…"

"If they can't get along without me for a little while, I don't know how to do my job anyway. Besides, I have a gift for you."

The way she was rubbing his growing erection was all the gift he needed. "I've got you. That's more than enough."

"I know, but remember how I asked you for your tattoo artist's information?"

She lowered his zipper, freeing him and cupping his balls. He couldn't see straight, much less think. "Yeah. You schedule me an appointment for something?"

Leaning closer, she whispered, "No. I scheduled one for me." She turned around, faced her desk, and let her wrap fall to the floor. A pair of black wings sprouted from her spine, the shading of the ink making them look as if they actually stood out from her body. And flames licked the tips of both wings, making them glow. "Do you like it?"

Dante reached forward and traced the tattoo with his fingers. It was some of the most intricate work he'd ever seen. "It's beautiful, but I thought you told me once that you didn't ever want a tattoo."

"That was the old me." Vicky shrugged, then reached

down and started inching the skirt of her dress higher and higher. "The old me was afraid of being dependent on a man. The new me...she wants everyone to know she belongs to the Inferno, that being with you makes me better, stronger. And she also wants him to take her on this desk right now and christen the office properly."

As the last words left her mouth, she stopped moving, her perfect ass on display before him as she bent over the top of her desk and spread her legs wide. There was no chance of him saying no. He stepped forward, easing between her slick folds and burying himself deep. There was nothing—*nothing*—that was going to keep him from being with his amazing woman another second.

Not the party in the other room.

And not even the ring burning a hole in his pocket.

Those things could wait.

Dante and Vicky couldn't. They'd already waited long enough.

Acknowledgments

The feeling of holding a new book in my hands and seeing my name on the cover never gets old, but there are so many more people than just me who deserve credit for getting the book to this point.

Janelle and Lola were invaluable. Between gangs and neighborhoods and getting from point A to point B...L.A. is almost a foreign country to me. Thank you both so much for not thinking my questions were stupid. Whoever runs the Twitter account for Pacific Park, I owe you, too. It was kind of a stupid question, but you answered me anyway. My amazing street team, the Renegades, for holding my hand as I battled with this book and my own self-doubt. You guys are the best people ever. Thanks for always having my back.

My editor, Karen, and all the other awesome people at Entangled have taught me so much. Thank you for putting up with my bouts of I-can't-itis. I am incredibly blessed to be surrounded by such fantastic people and be part of such an amazing company.

The biggest thank-you, however, goes to my family—especially my children. You two put up with my writerly insanity and support me no matter what. Every single day you remind me how important following this dream is. I hope when the time comes, it will have taught you that your own dreams are worth chasing, too. I love you.

About the Author

Julie Particka was told to get serious about her future in junior high. Several years after getting a bachelor's degree in chemistry, she realized being serious was overrated and went back to her first love—writing. Now rather than spending her days in the drudgery of the lab or teaching science to high school students, she disappears into worlds of her own creation where monsters sometimes roam, but true love still conquers all.

She can most often be located in the Detroit area with her favorite minions (the ones who know her as Mom), where she is currently hatching a plot for world domination. It involves cookies for everyone, so she's pretty sure there's no way it can fail…except the minions keep eating the cookies.

Discover the **Gone Hollywood** *series...*

TEMPTING HER FAKE FIANCÉ

Journalist Stasia Grant is in Vegas for the biggest interview of her career...and grappling with a broken heart, her cheating ex-husband, and a serious need for revenge. Her salvation comes from the most unlikely place—charming and sexy action star Evan Stone. After spending his life playing superhero, Evan has a plan for delicious satisfaction: a fake, week-long engagement and some no-strings fun to show Stasia's ex just what he's missing. Together, they're about to pull off the performance of a lifetime...but will they fall for their own con?

Also by Julie Particka

FALL WITH ME